Noah studied Laney.
"Why would her death be your fault?"

Her gaze dropped to her lap. "I was the big sister, the protector." Bitter regret whitewashed her pale cheeks. "It was my birthday. I wanted to have some fun, and my fun cost my sister her life. What a selfish little fool!"

"Aww, Laney." Noah reached a hand across the desk, though it couldn't go far enough to touch her. "You have no idea how many times I've heard stories like that from family members looking for someone to blame. Quite often themselves. You were just a kid being a kid."

Laney's hard expression shattered, and she sobbed. Tears flowed down her face and dripped off her chin. "I hope–" she hiccupped "–one day...I can believe that."

Blinking away the sting behind his eyes, Noah surged to his feet and grabbed a tissue from the box on his credenza. He came around his desk and sat in the guest chair beside her. She took the tissue and scrubbed as if she would wipe away memories.

"I hope you do take those words to heart. They're real and true." Noah brushed the back of her hand with his fingertips.

Books by Jill Elizabeth Nelson

Love Inspired Suspense

Evidence of Murder
Witness to Murder
Calculated Revenge

JILL ELIZABETH NELSON

writes what she likes to read—faith-based tales of adventure seasoned with romance. By day she operates as housing manager for a seniors' apartment complex. By night she turns into a wild and crazy writer who can hardly wait to jot down all the exciting things her characters are telling her, so she can share them with her readers. More about Jill and her books can be found at www.jillelizabethnelson.com. She and her husband live in rural Minnesota, surrounded by the woods and prairie and their four grown children who have settled nearby.

CALCULATED REVENGE

Jill Elizabeth Nelson

Steeple
Hill®

Published by Steeple Hill Books™

STEEPLE HILL BOOKS

Steeple
Hill®

ISBN-13: 978-0-373-67411-4

CALCULATED REVENGE

And when you stand praying, if you hold anything against anyone, forgive him, so that your Father in Heaven may forgive you your sins.

—*Mark* 11:25

To the heroic men and women, both civilian and law enforcement, who devote their time and energy to finding the lost and stolen little ones. May their hearts be wise, their arms be strong, and their ears be open to guidance from the supernatural God who loves the children better than any natural parent.

ONE

The grimy backpack rested abandoned against the playground fence. Laney Thompson's eyes riveted on the schoolbag, but her feet stuck to the gravel near the swings. What was the matter with her? The students had rushed less than a minute ago into the elementary school building after noon recess. One of them must have forgotten the bag. Simple explanation. Then why did her skin pebble as if she stood on this Minnesota playground in mid-January, rather than the balmy end of May?

A warm breeze puffed a curtain of light brown hair in front of her face, and she blinked, breaking the hold of the strange paralysis. Laney brushed the hair aside and moved forward. Standing in front of the pack, she curled her hands into fists. *Come on, pick it up.* But her arms balked at the command to reach for the pack's frayed top strap.

Dread pummeled her.

She studied the object. Mildew stains spattered the canvas, and the original color was barely discernable as green. Whoever owned this schoolbag had been mighty careless with it or was too poor to afford a new one. Several students who fit either description passed through her mind.

All she needed to do was check inside for papers identifying the owner. The plumpness of the pack suggested that there ought to be plenty of clues inside. She reached for the strap, then froze, breath sawing in her lungs. Blackness trimmed her vision.

Laney Thompson, this is no time for a panic attack. You left those behind. Remember?

Yes, she remembered the years of counseling. Vividly. Then the determined struggle to put the past behind her and get a college education—an effort prolonged and complicated by a mistake of a marriage and the birth of a beautiful daughter. But at twenty-eight she now had her teaching degree. She was what she had always dreamed of being—a protector and guide to the young. Perhaps to atone for…

Laney swallowed and rubbed damp palms against her tan slacks. She snatched up the pack. A side seam gave way, and the corner of a notebook stuck out. The bag was in worse shape than she'd realized. Laney squatted and set the pack on new spring grass. A smell like rancid musk wafted from the canvas. Her heart rattled against her ribs. Trembling fingers worked the zipper and another seam parted as she yanked the notebook out.

She had to know who owned this schoolbag.

Laney flipped open a yellowed page, and found a first name printed in ragged block letters in the top right corner. For breathless seconds, her mind denied what she saw. Then the horror—and the guilt—deluged her, as suffocating as the day of Laney's tenth birthday. The day the nightmare began.

Grace Thompson. The name mocked her from the page.

This backpack had belonged to her eight-year-old sister. At least, that's how old Gracie had been the day she disappeared on her way home from school. Alone. Eighteen years ago.

That terrible smell now held no mystery. Decay. She gagged. The pack had come from the unknown tomb where Gracie's abductor had stashed her body. Her killer had put the bag here on purpose. He wanted Laney to find it. To know he was nearby.

She scooted backward, wails ripping through her mind, but bottled in her chest. She tumbled onto her side and gripped her legs in a fetal position. The screams burst free.

A sliver of her mind continued to churn questions. Was he watching? Enjoying her breakdown? Why now? What did he want? Or who?

Briana!

A vision of her daughter's face sobered her like a plunge in a glacial lake. She sat up stiff. How could this mean anything else? Briana was newly eight years old. Just like Gracie.

Excited voices that had been there, but unregistered, reached her ears. The aide from the music department stuck his face in hers. "Are you all right?"

She surged to her feet, strong-arming him aside. "My daughter. I have to go!"

Astonished faces melted away before her as she charged between approaching people. Why couldn't she move faster than the speed of sludge? Laney yanked open the door and raced up a hallway floored in wax-coated linoleum and walls covered with bulletin boards and glass display cases. Familiar scents pumped through her nostrils—white-board markers, sweaty gym shoes stored in lockers. She rounded a corner and dodged around a line of kindergarteners and their teacher heading for the restrooms. Squeaks of surprise followed her into the first classroom on the left.

Briana's teacher and Laney's best friend, Ellen Kline, stood at the head of the third grade classroom. She stopped midsentence and stared at Laney. "What's going on?"

"Mommy!" A little girl's voice drew Laney's attention.

"Sweetie, you're okay!" She ran to her daughter at her desk and hugged her tight. At the smell of strawberry shampoo in soft, brown pigtails, she exhaled a thankful prayer.

"Mommy...I can...hardly breathe."

Laney loosened her grip and eased away from her daughter. Briana's sea-blue eyes, mirrors of her own, brimmed with puzzlement. The class-room was dead silent. They must all think she'd gone insane. She needed to find a quick excuse for the interruption without alarming her daughter, or anyone else, further.

Fastening a smile to her lips, Laney rose. "I'm sorry—I… Well, I just needed to check on my daughter. One of those mother's intuition things. I'm glad I was wrong." She nodded toward Ellen, whose puckered brow said she wasn't buying the lame explanation. "Forgive the interruption." She backed toward the door, and a soft buzz of student voices followed her out into the hall. So did Ellen.

Her friend stepped in front of her, hands planted on generous hips. "Are you okay?"

Laney's fingers dug into the soft flesh of Ellen's upper arms. "Don't take your eyes off Briana. Don't let her go anywhere alone, not even to the bathroom. I've got to see Principal Ryder, and then I'm going to call the police."

"The po—"

"I'll explain later." Laney hustled off, leaving her friend with her mouth open.

Seconds later, Laney burst through the door of the main office.

Miss Aggie, the receptionist, fixed her with an eagle's stare. "If you were a student, you'd risk a warning for running in the halls."

"Is he in?" Laney's breath came in little puffs.

"Who? Mr. Ryder?" Miss Aggie stood, her lined

face beginning to mirror the alarm Laney radiated from her whole body.

"What's up?" The man himself stepped out of the office situated to the left of the reception desk.

Lean and medium tall, the strength of Principal Ryder's steady green gaze left no one in doubt of his authority. In the school year that he and Laney had served the district together, he'd shown himself to be a man as protective of his students as he was a firm, but understanding disciplinarian. He was also as honorable as he was good-looking, a combination that amazed Laney, based on past life experience.

A wave of warm comfort swept over her. She'd found a safe haven. Noah wouldn't let anything bad happen to Briana. Hot tears spilled down her face and a sob surged from her throat.

Laney Thompson's shattered expression shot a deep burn through Noah's gut. In his thirty-six years, he'd had reason to learn the difference between a minor emergency and a critical situation. This felt like the latter. He motioned her into his office. As she stumbled past the reception desk, Miss Aggie stuffed a tissue into her hand. Noah nodded appreciation to the woman who really ran the show around here, and then closed his office door.

"Have a seat," he told the attractive special education teacher who'd dogged his thoughts since he interviewed her for the position last summer.

She melted into a cloth-covered chair in front of

his desk, wiping at pale cheeks with the tissue. Her fine-boned chin quivered. He perched on the edge of his desk. If she keeled over, he'd just as soon catch her before she hit the floor.

"What's this all about?"

"Briana," she croaked. "My daughter. I think she's in danger."

"How so?" His spine prickled.

Her fingers white-knuckled the wooden arms of her chair. "I don't have time to go into detail, but I just found a backpack left on our playground that belonged to my sister Grace." Her slender neck contracted around a deep swallow. "Gracie was abducted and presumed murdered eighteen years ago. They never found her body. Briana's the same age as my sister was when she disappeared. I just…I can't… Nothing can happen to my daughter!" Her haunted blue gaze sifted him, searching for a promise of safety.

He'd seen that look too often not to be wary of its demand. He leaned back and crossed his arms. "Where is your daughter right now?"

"In her classroom. Ellen is watching out for her, but she doesn't know why."

"And where's the backpack?"

"Still on the playground. It was more important to make you aware that a maniac may be nearby, and then to call the police."

"You're doing everything right, Laney. Make your call." He patted the phone on his desk. "I'll go to the playground and secure the evidence, while Miss Aggie puts the staff on alert."

"Thank you. I'm so glad you're in charge of this school."

The husky gratitude sandpapered through Noah as he went into the reception area. He was nobody's savior. He'd proven that six years ago.

Agatha Nederleitner speared him with a stare. "Anyone can see that woman's in trouble. How are you going to help her?"

"We're going to help her," Noah answered, then briefed her on what Laney had told him.

The woman grasped the situation quickly, and Noah was grateful once again for this gem in the rough. The steel-haired brick of the office never soft-pedaled her opinion, but her sternness hid a marshmallow heart. She refused to plague the children with her last name, so she was the beloved Miss Aggie who packed an ounce of sugar into her scolds and stood firm as a rock while everyone's problems crashed against her. Today, she would need all her fortitude.

"Announce an orange alert over the intercom," Noah finished. "Then give Laney any assistance she needs. I'll wait for the authorities on the playground. Send someone to get me if you need me."

"Will do." Miss Aggie's blazing brown eyes telegraphed that Satan himself would have a hard time getting past her to do anyone harm in her school.

As he strode up the hall, the woman's platinum

tones issued the orange alert, the internal code for intruder watch. In the tiny town of Cottonwood Grove, Minnesota, people routinely left their cars running during the winter while they ran into the grocery store for milk, so his code system had seemed extreme to some. When he implemented it, he'd hoped never to use some of the alerts—especially this one. At least it wasn't an Amber Alert, the national code for a missing child.

Noah strode onto the playground. A small group of staff members hovered near the fence about a foot from an entrance gap. In the center of the huddle stood the custodian, Richard Hodge. The man cradled a bulky object in his arm while he rifled through it.

"All right, people." Noah smacked his palms together, and heads swiveled toward him. The custodian froze with his hand in the bag. "Thanks for coming out to help. Richard, please leave the pack on the ground. I'll take it from here."

With murmurs and shrugs, the group dispersed.

The custodian plunked the bag on the grass and backed away from it. "Just tryin' to see whose it was. Didn't recognize the name."

"Thank you, but it's not your worry. Head inside, but be aware that we are on orange alert."

Richard's prematurely lined face settled into a scowl. "Figured we couldn't end the school year without some kind of trouble." He clomped away.

Noah watched him go. For a thirtysomething

guy with most of his life ahead of him, a steady job and good benefits, the custodian had the dimmest outlook of anyone he knew. What was his story?

Shaking his head, Noah studied the bag. The backpack used to be green. He squatted down and took in the shabby condition and decaying seams. A few sheets of yellowed paper stuck out of the torn edges—aged but not pulped by exposure to the elements. Interesting. When the police arrived, he'd have to inform them the custodian had handled the bag, so they could get his fingerprints for elimination. Laney's, too.

Noah let out a soft growl and rose. Even after all this time, his thoughts fell into investigator mode. This situation was a trap for him in more ways than one.

"The authorities are on their way." Laney's mellow voice reminded him of one of those traps.

He turned to find her approaching. Her complexion had more color than when she all but collapsed in his office. Everything about her appealed to him, from the glossy brown hair bouncing against slender shoulders to her big blue eyes and gentle way with her special needs students. But he'd vowed never again to mix his professional life with his personal life.

She stopped beside him, the top of her head coming to his chin, which made her a petite five-two or so. "I think we're going to see both the sheriff and the city boys," she said, her gaze fixed on the backpack. She shuddered and hugged herself.

Noah bunched his fists and denied the impulse to hold her. The temptation would have been harder to squash if he didn't know so many eyes were on them. He'd seen noses pressed against the windows. Even without the orange alert, people in this small school could smell something was up.

"Tell me about it, Laney." He stepped close.

Noah mentally smacked himself for a fool. The fresh rain scent of her understated cologne reached his nostrils, and as usual, those enormous eyes did terrible, wonderful things to his insides. Good thing for him she'd always appeared oblivious to the attraction.

"Grace was autistic," she said. "It wouldn't have been hard for someone to take advantage of her."

"She was eight." He grimaced. "It's pretty easy for an adult to take advantage of any child that young."

"I know but…how do I explain?" She rubbed the side of her neck. "My sister didn't see the world in the same way as a child without that particular perspective. Gracie could fixate on something and not notice one other thing around her. The monster who took her must have lured her with something that fascinated her. Otherwise she was leery of strangers, and could get vocal and combative if someone unfamiliar invaded her space."

Noah frowned. "Lured her? You're sure it was a stranger abduction?"

"The FBI came to that conclusion after extensive investigation."

"Did the predator have to get her away from a public place? If he found her in a remote or private location, he wouldn't have cared if there was a struggle."

Laney's sable brows lifted. "You talk like someone familiar with these situations."

Noah rippled his shoulders. "A school principal needs to be these days."

She looked away, and a breath stuttered between her teeth. "The world has gotten so scary. You surmised correctly. Grace was walking home from school and disappeared from our home block. People were in their yards, but no one saw a thing."

"I take it she was never found."

"Not her body, just evidence that she didn't survive the abduction. A lot of blood was discovered in the bottom of a ravine near Grand Valley. That's the town in southeastern Minnesota where we lived at the time." She shook her head. "I blame myself to this day."

Noah narrowed his gaze at her. Why did she feel responsible? She couldn't have been much older than her sister. Just a kid.

A sheriff's SUV and a Cottonwood Grove police cruiser pulled up to the curb outside the playground fence, lights flashing but no sirens. Sheriff

Hank Lindoll and one of his deputies climbed out of the SUV, and a pair of city officers out of the car. The convocation strode toward them in V formation, with Lindoll flying point.

"Noah." The tall, rawboned sheriff greeted him and sent a long glance toward Laney.

"Hank." Noah nodded to the county official who'd be lead investigator in this case. A good man. He should feel relieved. Instead, he tamped down an irrational spike of resentment.

"What've we got here?" The sheriff glared at the tattered pack.

"Laney says it belonged to her sister who was abducted as a child. I'll let her fill you in."

Noah forced himself to back away as the sheriff started the interview process and assigned his deputy and the other officers to cordoning off the area for examination. Eyes would really be glued to school windows now that yellow tape was going up.

He went back to his office and found Miss Aggie fielding questions from alarmed staff. She told them he would issue a statement soon. Noah sent them to perform assignments around the buildings, then set up a game plan with Miss Aggie.

When Noah returned to the edge of the crime scene tape, the sheriff was on the phone.

Laney sidled up to him. "He's calling the FBI. The Minneapolis field office investigated Gracie's disappearance years ago. They've got the case file from back then."

He nodded. "They'll probably want to come out here."

She wrinkled her nose. "I hope they don't send the same people. One in particular."

Sheriff Lindoll smacked his phone shut. "A team of agents and Evidence Recovery Technicians are on their way from Minneapolis. The agent in charge said for us to hold the scene but not do anything until they arrive."

Noah nodded. "I can buy that for letting their techs get first shot at the schoolbag, but we need to contain the people factor." He canted his head toward the school building. "I want to meet with teaching staff first and give them every available detail. Then I'd like to hold a general assembly and explain things in simple terms that even the kids can grasp. We'll send them home with letters for their parents. Families should be on the alert if there's a child predator in the area."

Laney gasped. "But won't that frighten everybody, especially the kids?"

Noah met her concerned gaze. "People will be afraid, but not panicked. I believe they'll react with steady heads, even the children, if the information is presented the right way."

"And you're the guy to do that for sure," Sheriff Lindoll spoke up.

"And you're the guy to organize students and staff into interview groups while everyone is assembled," Noah shot back. "We need to speak to people while memories are fresh, before they've had time to go home and debrief with friends and family. Every class was on the playground in shifts over the noon hour before Laney found the pack. We need to find out if anyone saw someone leave it, or if and when people first started noticing the pack. That should help establish a timeline to narrow the investigation."

The sheriff pursed his lips. "That'll lean on FBI toes, but I think you've got a winner of a plan. Not surprising, with your background." He smacked Noah on the shoulder and tromped off to consult with his deputy.

With your background. Noah gritted his teeth. Hank *had* to mention that in front of Laney. But in this situation, wasn't it only a matter of time before his secret was out?

"I'll have Miss Aggie call the teachers together." Noah avoided Laney's questioning gaze. "I'd like you to be in that meeting and share the facts. Then you might want to pull your daughter aside and give her a heads-up on what's going on. You can stay with her in my private office until we call the assembly. Then I'll have you sit backstage so you can hear but not be seen. I don't want Briana subjected to staring eyes."

She touched his arm, and his gaze returned to hers. His pulse rate quickened. How could she not feel this powerful connection between them? *Please, don't let her feel it.*

"Thank you," she said. "You've been terrific. I knew you would be."

A smile quivered up at him, slipping a sharp pang of longing beneath the armor his head had erected around his heart. As far as he knew, there was no man in her life. Her ex-husband was out of the picture. She was available, but out of his reach. Not only was theirs a work relationship, but she was now the nexus of a missing person's investigation. Pure poison for him.

Noah answered her smile with an effort, then strode toward the school doors.

There was no way he could risk involvement with Laney, or this case, beyond his duties as school principal. *But,* a small voice niggled, *if there's a predator lurking near the students, shouldn't that include catching the slime?* He slowed his pace. He had the skills, and this incident involved him directly, but to save his sanity he had to let law enforcement handle this. After what happened six years ago, nothing could drag him back into the business.

TWO

Laney ushered her daughter into the office under the speculative gazes of a pair of aides loitering near the staff mailboxes. Miss Aggie stepped out from behind her desk, and her forbidding glare shooed the curious aides out the room. Then she turned a smile on Briana and motioned them into Noah's inner sanctum. Laney mustered a faint nod of thanks.

Her chest tightened as Miss Aggie closed the door. Laney looked down at her daughter. Now she'd have to tell her about Gracie. It had been difficult to go over the whole thing with the teaching staff a few minutes ago, but those were adults. How could she explain to an eight-year-old that she had an aunt she'd never heard about, much less what had happened to that child?

"Mama, what's wrong?" Briana's nostrils pinched above a frown.

Laney settled her daughter into one of the principal's guest chairs, then eased into the other one. "Bree, I have something to tell you."

"Is it bad, Mama?"

"Yes, honey, but it's about something that happened a long time ago. At least, it started then, but I think… I'm afraid… Oh, I don't know how to say this."

Briana's little hand folded around Laney's. "It's okay, Mama. You can tell me anything. We're BFFs."

"Best Friends Forever. Yes, we are." Laney wavered a smile at her daughter, whose open gaze radiated innocent trust. Silently, she cursed the evil that had again touched her life and now forced her to violate that innocence with vile news.

God, give me strength. Give me wisdom. She filled every air passage with fortifying oxygen. "I need to tell you a story about a little girl your age."

In halting, terse statements the tale came out. A flat, angry calm blanketed her words. Briana stared intent and silent into her face as she spoke. When she finished telling about Grace, Bree nodded, expression sober.

"I would have liked Grace." A soft smile flashed. "I'm excited to meet her in heaven."

"You would have liked her a lot, and you'll get the chance to meet her one day." Laney got down on her knees and hugged her sweet daughter, then put her at arm's length. "But that's not the end of the story. Today I— Well, I found something that lets me know that the bad man is back. We need to do certain things to stay safe until he's caught. That's why Mr. Ryder let us be in his office."

Briana's eyes widened. "Principal Ryder's going to look out for us?"

"In a way. He's arranging things with people in the school so everyone can be safe."

Briana nodded. "That's good. I like Principal Ryder."

"Yes, we can trust him." She'd only known Noah Ryder for this school year, but she knew that with every fiber of her being. Besides, he couldn't have planted the backpack. He wasn't outside during recess today.

Laney tweaked her daughter's button nose. "But remember, we can't trust strangers. I need you to stay with me every minute. Don't get out of my sight. And if you can't be with me, I'll make sure you're with someone who will take care of you. Do exactly what they say."

"Don't worry, Mama." Her daughter patted Laney's cheek. "God's watching over us."

The depth of faith in the simple statements stole Laney's breath. Where was her faith? It sure wasn't very strong in this area. She struggled to believe God would—not could—keep them safe from this monster? Why hadn't He protected Gracie?

Why didn't you? A small voice accused.

A rap on the door brought her head around. Noah sidled halfway inside. His questioning stare met hers.

Laney rose. "You shouldn't have to knock to enter your own office."

"Just wanted to make sure I wasn't intruding at a bad moment."

"No, we're done here."

"You okay, princess?" His gaze fell toward Briana, who beamed at him. As usual, Noah had said exactly the right thing. Bree's pink princess pajamas were her favorite.

"I'm fine, Mr. Ryder." The little girl hopped up. "Mama told me about my Auntie Grace and the bad man who's come back." She stepped toward the principal, face tilted up toward him. "I'm glad you're gonna help keep us safe."

Noah rendered a half smile. "I'll do my best." He looked toward Laney. "Everyone's gathering in the gymnasium. I'll escort you to a secure location backstage."

"We're ready." Laney nodded, not at all sure she'd spoken the truth.

She snagged her daughter's hand and followed on Noah's heels. As always, his presence enveloped her like a warm security blanket, and she craved more of that feeling. Too bad the principal had made it clear, by fending off more than one unwed teacher's batted eyelashes, that he wasn't interested in a work romance, even though there was no rule against it.

They wove through a hallway teeming with children and adults headed for the gym, which doubled as an auditorium in this small school. The masses parted before the school principal, and

Laney kept herself and Briana closely in his wake. She caught snatches of agitated speculation in conversations buzzing around her. Soon they went through a doorway and entered the relative calm of the stairwell that gave backstage access. As they climbed the few stairs, the faint scent of resin-coated boards greeted her. Two folding chairs waited in the left wing area between the heavy, velvet curtains. A city police officer hovered nearby.

"I'll leave you in Deputy Carlson's capable hands," Noah told them with a nod toward Laney and a wink at Briana, who warbled a tiny giggle.

"Thank you," Laney breathed.

Something in her expression must have betrayed that she hovered between petrified and panicked, because he laid his hands on her shoulders. His solid nearness drew her. What would he think if he knew how tempted she was to throw herself into his arms? She kept her gaze averted. Maybe he wouldn't notice the pulse pumping in her throat.

"You're doing great, Laney," he said. Then he leaned closer. His warm breath feathered the hair on the top of her head. "Hang tough. We're going to get through this."

She lifted her head, but he'd already turned away. Did he say *we?* Just how much could she presume on this man?

Laney watched Noah Ryder walk out onto the

stage. The muted roar of conversation dimmed, and at his first words, halted.

Butterflies fluttered around inside Laney's stomach. In a few minutes, every student and staffer would know about the greatest tragedy of her life—a tragedy that now cast a shadow over theirs. In a few hours, the entire town would know. If the flourishing local grapevine hadn't accomplished that task already.

Who did this murderous pervert think he was? Why had he returned to plague her now, after all these years? How could she, or anyone, possibly keep her daughter safe?

Laney sank onto one of the chairs and pulled Briana onto her lap, hugging her close. Officer Carlson nodded approval. No doubt he assumed she meant to offer comfort to her daughter when the opposite was closer to the truth. Only one of them was trembling, and it wasn't the child.

Thirty-five minutes after his presentation about what had occurred and its significance for everyone present, Noah finished interviewing the third grade class. The children sat cross-legged on the gym floor with their teachers. Some of the little faces were pale, some flushed—depending on whether they considered this situation frightening or exciting.

Noah thanked the group and unfolded himself from the floor where he'd gotten down on their level to ask his questions. He consulted his notes as he headed for Sheriff Lindoll, who was speaking with a group of sixth graders. So far, the feedback indicated that the backpack had not been on the playground during the first half of recess period when grades kindergarten through three were outside.

The sheriff turned away from his group and met Noah in the middle of the gym floor. "I've got credible positives on the bag being seen by students and teachers during the second recess period."

Noah nodded. "I've got the opposite with the younger group. It looks like either the bag was placed during the ten minutes between recess periods or when grades four to six were on the grounds."

"Sounds reasonable."

"Has anyone reported seeing who left it?"

"Negative. But we're not done talking to people."

"Yes, you are," sniped a voice from the past.

Spine stiff, Noah swiveled toward the last man on the planet he ever wanted to see again. "Hello, Special Agent Justin Burns."

The sheriff's brows flew up. Was it because Noah knew the FBI agent or because he hadn't done too well at keeping the sneer out of his tone? Burns hadn't changed much. Looming middle age had drawn a few more creases on his bulldog face, but the frost-gray eyes were still as cold as a gravestone. As usual, he wore a crisp-pressed suit that made him look like a surly, burly version of Tommy Lee Jones in *Men in Black*. And the set of his pencil mouth…well, the urge to knock the arrogant expression off that mug hadn't diminished with time.

"It's *Supervisory* Special Agent now," Burns said, his sneer not hidden, either. "What are you doing here, Ryder? I thought you were retired from bungling investigations."

Make that urge a compulsion…suppressed. Barely. This time.

Noah stretched his lips into a smile that was as good as a spit. "Tread lightly, Burns. You're on my territory, and my students' best interests *will* be served."

"This is our school principal." Hank plunked a hand onto Noah's shoulder.

Burns barked a laugh. "Nurse-maiding the kiddies, are we?" He turned his attention toward the sheriff. "Make no mistake. We are in charge. We'll collect whatever information your people have gathered and take the investigation from here. You'll be informed whenever we need information from you on a local matter, but this case reaches beyond Cottonwood Grove."

The sheriff's gaze met Noah's. He sent Hank a miniscule shrug.

"I can take your team to the backpack," the sheriff said to Burns.

"No need. The ERTs are already examining the bag and the site. We recognize crime scene tape when we see it."

"Hooray for the good guys." Noah looked around the gym. Other agents were joining interview groups or consulting with the city officers. Some even deigned to smile and joke with the local yokels. At least the rest of this federal team didn't have their ties yanked too tight. Most of them weren't even wearing one. Or a suit, either. He returned his gaze to Burns. "I wonder if you're the one."

The agent drew himself up to his full height, which was a good couple of inches shorter than Noah. "The one what?"

"Miss Thompson mentioned an agent that was involved in the original investigation."

"Would that be Laney Thompson, the victim's sister? Where is she? She's got questions to answer."

"She and her daughter are backstage. Come with me." If this guy got out of line with Laney, he'd stop curbing his impulses, even if the swing got him jail time.

"That was very good, sweetie," Laney told her daughter, who gazed up proudly from the book she was reading aloud.

"Laney Thompson, I need to talk to you!"

The hairs at the base of her neck stood on end as

if someone had scraped fingernails across the chalkboard of her mind. Those growled tones were from a long-ago nightmare. She looked up to see Noah, with Special Agent Burns in tow, bearing down on her.

The FBI agent stopped in front of their chairs. "Supervisory Special Agent Justin Burns. I'm told you remember me." He spoke as if her recollection of him was a matter of pride.

It had taken her a long time to overcome the nightmares featuring the agent's roughshod interrogation of her as a traumatized child. Burns would have to trample her dead body to do the same thing to Briana.

Laney rose and stared the agent in his pug nose. "What would you like to know? But leave my daughter out of it. This is the first she's heard about what happened back then, and she wasn't anywhere near Gracie's schoolbag."

Burns looked from Briana back to her. "All grown up and with a kid of your own. We'll see where the investigation takes us. Is there somewhere we can visit in private?" The agent pointed a look toward Noah, who stood with his arms away from his body, legs slightly apart, as if he'd as soon tackle Burns as look at him.

They glared at one another like familiar enemies. Burns must have worked fast to get on Noah's bad side so quickly. Then again, the agent had that gift.

"You can use my office," Noah said. "I'll escort you."

"No need." Burns waved him off. "I'm sure Laney knows where it is."

"Ms. Thompson." Laney spoke in unison with Noah. They shared a look, and sparkly fizz shot through her middle at the smile in his eyes. What was the matter with her? Now was so not the time for this hopeless attraction to her boss.

Burns's jaw firmed. "Very well, Ms. Thompson. Lead the way. And you," he turned and jabbed a finger toward Noah, "stay out of this investigation."

Laney drew herself up. "Stay out of this investigation? If your people find any lead worth following it will likely be because of this man's quick thinking. He secured the scene, alerted the school, organized the interviews—"

"You did what?" Burns put himself in Noah's personal space. "I might have known you couldn't keep your nose out of where it doesn't belong. I told the sheriff not to make a move until we arrived."

"How can you be so obtuse?" Laney burst out. "We need a vicious murderer apprehended, and you instruct your fellow law officer not to employ his intellect, training or experience?" Both men were staring at her now. She was babbling in English-nerdese, but she was on a roll. "If Sheriff Lindoll had listened to you instead of Noah, you'd be hours behind on an investigation that is now well in hand. Accolades are more in order than scorn. And," she sniffed, "if you need a dictionary to look up any of my verbiage, this school is gifted with an abundance of those."

"Mommy?" A tap on her side brought her attention to her daughter, who stood clutching her book. "He can use a dictionary from my classroom."

Silence blanketed the moment, except for the background noise of voices from the gymnasium. A snort turned everyone's heads. Officer Carlson stood red-faced and grinning from his post behind the folding chairs. A suppressed chuckle came from Noah, whose lips had disappeared between his teeth.

Laney tugged a lock of her daughter's hair. "Thank you, sweetie. You're a thoughtful little girl." Her heart was galloping like a colt let out of the gate. She'd just thoroughly antagonized the man who held the authority in a life or death investigation involving her family. *Great going, girl.* She tried, but an apology wouldn't form in her mouth. The man was a grade-A blockhead, but they were stuck with him.

Burns's subzero gaze surveyed her as if she was a speck of lint. "If your sophomoric tantrum is quite finished, you and I have matters to discuss. And I do want to speak to the child, as well."

"My daughter's name is Briana." She turned her focus on her little girl. "Briana, this is Agent Burns of the Federal Bureau of Investigation. Your mommy set a very bad example. We need to respect his authority and position."

Briana smiled and held out her hand to the agent. "Pleased to meet you, Agent Burns."

The agent stared at the hand as if he'd been offered a porcupine. Then he slowly took the little member in his. "Good meeting you, too, Briana." The words came out a bit gruff, but his expression softened.

Noah dipped his head, as if chastened. "I was going to offer to be present during the interview, but I think you can take care of yourself." He looked at his watch. "I need to arrange for parents and bus drivers to be aware of late school dismissal." With a small wave, he left the stage in one direction, while Laney motioned Burns to follow her in the other.

On the way to Noah's office, questions bombarded her mind. What had Burns meant by his statement that he "might have known" Noah couldn't stay out of the investigation? Had the agent and the principal met before? How? When? And why did the local police chief respect Noah's advice about the investigation? Who was Noah Ryder, really? The internal gossip den contained sketchy knowledge about the man's background. He started his teaching career about five years ago in a different school system, then got his principal's license and took over in Cottonwood Grove two years ago. What had he done before that?

When they arrived at the reception area, Burns dismissed Officer Carlson, and then swept past Miss Aggie without a glance as he took over the lead into the principal's inner sanctum. He made himself at home in Noah's big desk chair, pulled a small tape recorder from his pocket and placed it on the edge of the desk. Laney and Briana occupied the guest chairs.

It took only a few minutes for Laney to divulge the story about finding the school bag on the playground, though she kept the panic attack to herself. Burns was a cold, hard facts kind of guy, and she didn't need to expose her shattered emotions.

Burns spent a few minutes grilling her, then he turned his attention to Briana. "Young lady, have you noticed anyone watching you these past few days or weeks? A stranger? Or someone who shouldn't be paying you that much attention? Think very hard now. This is important."

Briana's brows scrunched together, and she kicked her feet back and forth. Then she shook her head, pigtails flapping.

The agent leaned across the desk. "You're sure. No one when you're outside? Or with friends? Or with your mother somewhere? At the store, perhaps?"

"No one," Briana answered in a small voice.

"How about the playground where the bag was found? Someone watching—"

"Agent Burns," Laney interrupted, "my daughter has already said no."

"Yes!" her daughter burst out.

They both gaped at her.

Briana bounced in her seat. "There was a man in a suit." She screwed up her mouth. "I remember 'cuz I noticed him when my friend Alicia lost her pinky ring under the slide."

"A man in a suit." Burns all but sprawled across the desk. "He was watching you?"

"No, not me."

"Bree," Laney said, "why didn't you report this? We're not supposed to let strangers hang around the playground. Haven't you learned anything from the lessons Mr. Ryder's put on about stranger awareness?" Her tone had gone shrill before she finished the sentence.

Her daughter's lower lip quivered. "But Mommy, he didn't have mean eyes. More like sad. And he went away as soon as the bell rang and we had to go inside."

"What did the man look like?" The agent's palm slapped the desktop.

Laney fried him with a glare. "You are not interrogating a criminal."

"All right. Okay." He lifted his hands and settled back in his chair. "Briana," he gritted between a wooden smile, "would you kindly describe this person to me?"

The little girl shrugged. "He had a suit on, but not the same color as yours. His hair was dark, except for white spots here." She motioned toward her temples. "And the metal pole on the fence came to here on him." She sawed her hand back and forth across her upper abdomen.

"Very good, honey." Laney squeezed her daughter's arm, then looked at Burns. "The stabilizing pole is about halfway up the fence. That would make our man less than average height—five foot eight or so."

The man grunted. "Good description, young lady. Now would you mind going with one of my agents while I talk to your mom for a little while?"

Laney shook her head. "I won't send her with someone she doesn't know. I want my friend Ellen to be with them."

Burns hissed out a breath. "Make it happen, but my guy will be in charge. Unless you think one of my agents is the perp." His sarcasm was sharp enough to scrape paint.

He retrieved a radio from his belt while Laney went to the office door and peered out. The outer area teemed with people, and Miss Aggie was busy at a swamped desk. Some of those hanging around were bus drivers. Laney glanced at the wall clock. School was overdue to be dismissed. On the other side of the area, a tall, dark-haired man waved to her, flashing a big smile. It was Pierce Mayfield, driver of the small city bus that transported several in-town children to and from school. Laney answered with a flutter of the fingers.

Pierce had been flirting with her all year and

even asked her out a couple of times. So far she'd turned him down. Not that Pierce wasn't nice. He was even pretty good-looking. His eyebrows of slightly different heights and vaguely crooked nose gave him an appealingly interesting face. He simply wasn't a certain school principal who had already captured her attention. Of course, she might do well to give up that hopeless quest and give Pierce a chance. Ellen sure thought so. She'd been trying to get them together all year. And Laney was all for finding a good husband. Briana deserved the daddy she kept praying for…but first, her precious little girl needed to be safe.

A welcome figure stepped into the reception area. Now she didn't have to ask Miss Aggie to call over the intercom.

"Ellen!" Laney motioned her friend over.

"Oh, girl!" Ellen swept her into big arms, and her lavender scent enveloped Laney.

For a brief instant, she allowed herself to slump into the comfort. Then she pulled away. "Can you go with this agent," she pointed to the big fellow in a sport coat who'd come up behind Ellen, "and look after Briana?"

"Anything." Ellen's brown eyes poured warm honey over Laney. "We'll hang out in my classroom."

"Thanks. You're the best." Laney squeezed her friend's hand and called for Briana. "You remember what I told you about minding anyone watching out for you."

"I will, Mama."

The little girl skipped off, holding Ellen's hand and trailed by Hulk Hogan's clone with a buzz cut.

Laney closed the office door and returned to her hot seat in front of Agent Burns.

The agent studied her with flat eyes. "What do you know about Ryder?"

"What's that got to do with this situation?"

Burns stared at her like a hawk at a mouse.

Laney shifted in her seat and crossed her legs. "He's a terrific school principal."

"That's it?"

"I've only been here one school term. It's not like we hang out socially." Not that she wouldn't like to, but that was none of Burns's business.

The agent twirled a paper clip between his thumb and forefinger. "Don't place any confidence in him to figure this out for you. Leave that to the professionals."

Laney blinked at him. What in the world was he getting at?

A knock sounded at the door.

"Come!" Burns called.

A short man walked in carrying a box about the size of a microwave oven. Laney recognized the strap of Grace's backpack sticking out the top inside a clear plastic bag.

"This is Agent Wallace," Burns said. "One of our Evidence Recovery Technicians. I need you to take a look at the items from your sister's backpack and tell us if you notice anything out of place or missing."

"O-okay," Laney quavered. Nausea churned her insides.

Wallace began taking bagged and tagged items out of the box and laying them carefully on any available surface. First, the empty pack itself. Then papers and notebooks and pencils and erasers, a ruler, an assortment of hair pins, a shriveled and barely recognizable candy bag, a smashed calculator and several school texts and workbooks.

"That's it?" Burns grated.

"All she wrote," Wallace confirmed.

"I see nothing out of place." Laney walked around and forced herself to examine every object. "Even the candy is her favorite—Reese's Pieces." A lump crowded into her throat and tears stung her eyes. *Oh, Gracie!* She swallowed the lump and took a deep breath. "What's this dark stuff staining the corner of the bag and this book? It's not—" She didn't finish the statement, as her brain registered the truth without needing to hear from the technician.

Her sister's lifeblood.

Her gut heaved, and she hurried from the room. No one tried to stop her. She dodged between people in the crowded reception area. Her foot rammed something hard, and she stumbled. Righting herself, she looked down to see heavy, brown work boots. Must be steel-toed. Then she looked up into the scowling face of the custodian, Richard Hodge. His glower chilled her heated rush.

"Pardon me," she murmured.

The man sneered and turned away.

Laney stared at his stiff, broad back. Why did the custodian dislike her? She shook her head and moved on, grief surging behind her eyes. A headache began to throb. She needed to get somewhere alone. Just for a few minutes.

She reached the exit, but a hand closed around her arm and turned her.

"Pierce. Hi. I can't talk right now. I'm going—"

"Wherever it is, consider me your escort." His concerned brown gaze drew a trickle from a corner of her eye. "Hey!" His thumb wiped at the tear.

She ducked her head. "I'm sorry. I don't think you can go with me to the restroom." She escaped out the door of the office.

In the hallway, students were rushing around, getting ready to head for home. Locker doors rattled, and juvenile voices yelled greetings and banter. Familiar sounds. Comforting sounds. Even the threat of a nameless stalker couldn't douse the kids' spirits on a fine day this close to summer break. Laney moved quickly between them, forcing herself to bestow smiles.

Fellow staff members called encouragement like, "We're with you, Laney," and shot her thumbs-up. But she read from their eyes that they didn't know how to guarantee a good outcome any more than she did. Their sense of safety had been violated along with hers. At last she reached the ladies' room and scurried past people to the last stall. She darted inside, closed the door, and leaned her aching head against the cool metal.

Oh, God, let this be a dream.

But it wasn't, and she couldn't turn back today's clock any more than she could have turned it back eighteen years ago and made a different choice on that awful day.

THREE

Noah found Laney in her darkened classroom slumped at her desk with damp paper towels pressed to her forehead. He cleared his throat so he wouldn't startle her as he approached. "The children are gone for the day, but Ellen has Briana. They're playing a game."

"I know." She looked up, fathoms of pain in her shadowed gaze. "She's a good friend. She's been giving me some space to process."

"Is it working?" He knew the answer before he asked. This woman needed an old-fashioned bawl session, but he'd leave that to Ellen Kline's sturdy shoulder. It was not a good idea for him to put his arms around Laney Thompson. He had to maintain professional distance, even in his thoughts. Too bad that plan wasn't working very well.

Laney wadded the paper towels and chucked the ball across the room. She made the wastebasket.

"Good arm," he said.

"Are they still here?"

"The FBI? Yes, they've commandeered a meeting room. Agent Burns said to tell you he'd have someone outside your apartment all night."

Laney snorted. "So you're his errand boy now? I suppose he shared that information so that I won't call the cops on his agent."

Noah sent her a wry smile. "He plays it close to the vest."

"A bit too close." She told him what Briana had confessed to Agent Burns about noticing a man in a suit lurking outside the playground just before the end of second and third grade recess.

He rubbed his chin. "That fits with the timeline for the first appearance of the backpack."

Laney pressed a hand to her chest. "I hope this is finally a break in the case, but I'm not holding my breath. Agent Burns wasn't in charge of the team when Gracie went missing, but he was there, throwing his weight around. They didn't find anything then. Why should I believe results will be different now?"

"A hot new lead can sometimes break a cold case."

Laney leaned back in her chair, her gazed fixed on him. Noah shifted his stance and looked around the room. If décor was a reflection of personality, this room did Laney justice. Everything from the skipping hippos stenciled on the wall to the bright construction paper flowers edging the bulletin board spoke of warmth and energy. This was a great room for mentally and physically challenged kids to find safe stimulation, as well as hearty doses of encouragement.

"Why do I get the feeling you know a lot about criminal investigations?" She asked the question Noah wished he hadn't invited with his careless remark.

He sent her a casual smile. "A hobby of mine."

Her eyes widened. "You investigate crimes in your spare time?"

"I meant that it's an interest." Beads of moisture sprang up beneath the collar of his polo shirt. How close was that kernel of truth to telling a lie? "I've got a suggestion," he hurried on. "It's Friday tomorrow. Why don't you and Briana take the day off? Then you'll have the whole weekend to stay home and regroup. You probably have people to contact."

"My parents."

"Of course. Maybe by Monday things will have cooled down here. And maybe we'll even have a dirtbag in a suit behind bars."

"How I hope so!" She rose. "Thank you." She came around the desk and touched his arm. "I'll take you up on your offer."

"I'll check on you, at least by phone, every day."

"I appreciate your concern." Her smile emerged and did amazing things to his insides.

"Let me walk you to your car. We can pick up Briana on the way."

They collected the little girl, and the child slipped one hand into her mother's and took Noah's with the other. The simple intimacy felt too right to be comfortable. By the time Noah waved Laney and Briana off toward home, he was sweating in earnest, and not from the balmy weather.

He returned to the office, where Miss Aggie was closing up shop.

"You did well today," she said.

"Thanks. So did you."

She walked to the door, then turned and lasered him with a look. "But remember, some gains are worth great risk. Don't screw up your chance at a future because of the past."

She whisked away, leaving Noah with his mouth open. What did she mean by that remark? Had some little birdie with a sheriff's badge been twittering in her ear, or was his attraction to Laney as obvious as his efforts to keep her at arm's length?

Noah undid a button on his shirt and retired to the inner office, where he got on the phone. "Have you been talking out of turn, Lindoll?" he said as soon as Hank came on the line.

"Huh?"

"Did you tell my secretary who I was?"

"Are you kidding? I haven't told a soul, but I'm tempted to spill the beans to Laney Thompson. She could use your services right now."

"Nothing doing. I'm retired and into my second

career, which I like very much, thank you. Besides, she's got *you* on her side."

The sheriff snorted. "Fat lot of good that'll do her when my people are shut out of the investigation. Information is a one-way street with this Burns, except for something he deems 'local' enough for us to know."

"And you think I'd fare any better? You saw how we get along."

"Must be a story there, eh?" The man gave a dry chuckle.

"Later. Maybe. Right now, I'm calling to see if anything more came of the interviews your guys conducted. Is there anything I need to know to protect my students and staff?"

Several heartbeats passed. Noah's internal antennae perked up. There was something, but Hank must not be sure if it was significant or not.

"We do have one suspicious circ," the sheriff finally said.

"Suspicious circumstance? Involving who?"

"Glen Crocker, a local electrician, has been missing for a couple of days."

Noah pursed his lips. "The timing would be right for a perp who needed to go somewhere and get that backpack."

The sheriff sighed. "I'd hate to see this turn out to be a local guy. Could be Glen's just skipped out on his family, which is bad enough. Let me look up the report. My deputy got this lead at the school from the guy's son and interviewed the wife at home."

Noah doodled with an automatic pencil while he listened to papers rustle at the other end. "Glen must be Sam Crocker's dad. Sam's in Mrs. Link's fifth grade class."

"You sure know your students…and their families. That's part of what makes you a good principal, but paying attention to people also makes you an outstanding investigator."

"Get off it, Hank." Noah stabbed the pencil point into the pad.

"All right, but I'm just saying. Ah, here it is." A desk chair creaked in the background. "According to little Sam, his daddy left for a job day before yesterday, and the kid hasn't seen him since. My deputy talked to the mom, and she didn't know where her husband was, either. Didn't seem too surprised Glen took off, which is why she hadn't reported him missing." Hank snorted. "Must've been problems in the marriage."

"That's too bad." Noah shook his head. "Especially for little Sam. Any personal effects gone from this guy's home?"

"His Chevy Impala's gone, but he didn't grab any of his clothes or belongings. Doesn't mean he didn't take a hike of his own free will, so maybe this has nothing to do with our sicko on the loose. Glen's been a citizen in good standing around here for a decade, but I've initiated inquiries about him prior to coming to Cotton-wood Grove."

"Sounds good. And I've got something for you that I'll bet Burns hasn't gotten around to sharing." Noah gave the sheriff the information Laney had shared about the man in the suit watching kids on the playground.

"Hmm. The description doesn't match Crocker. Thanks for the lead though."

"And you're going to call me if you find out anything interesting?" The doodles became larger and darker.

Hank laughed. "Do you really want me to, Mr. Principal? I can practically feel the investigator salivating."

The lead on the end of the pencil snapped. "Just call me."

"Will do." The sheriff hung up, still chuckling.

Was it really too much to ask to be kept in the loop about something that could affect a whole school full of children in his care? Noah snatched up a fistful of paperwork Miss Aggie had left for him to sign. Taking part in the investigation was the last thing on his mind. It was!

Laney struggled through the evening at home in their apartment. She and Briana did the regular things—homework, a select amount of TV time, supper, a bedtime book—but everything felt odd and ill-fitting, as if ordinary had skewed off its axis. By the time Bree knelt at her bedside in her pink princess pajamas for prayers, Laney's headache had morphed into Goliath stomping through her brain. At least she'd managed to give Briana a normal evening.

"… and, Jesus, remember that I'm still waiting for a daddy. And please help Mama to get her real smile back…"

Laney tuned in to her daughter's conversation with the Lord.

"… and not be sad about her sister and not be so a-scared. Amen."

Then Briana hopped up and threw her arms around Laney. She squeezed her daughter extra tight. What a reminder that kids were more perceptive than adults realized. She hadn't done as great with her stick-to-routine plan as she'd thought.

Laney tucked Briana under the covers. "Would you like to talk about what happened today?"

Her daughter shook her head, a peaceful smile on the heart-shaped face that was a miniature of her own. "I talked to God. Everything's going to be all right."

Laney kissed Briana's forehead. "I'll count on it, then."

Briana settled in with a contented sigh. "I think I'm real close to getting my daddy," she murmured.

Laney's pulse jumped, but she didn't answer, just shut off the bedroom light and left the door ajar. She didn't have the heart to discourage her little girl with the information that her mother had no daddy material on her social calendar.

Then she went through the apartment and checked the security of every window and the front door. Locked up tight. In the bathroom, she downed a couple of painkillers. The phone rang, and she hurried to the living room. Her fingers hesitated over the receiver. She didn't recognize the number on the caller ID. That monster wouldn't dream of calling her, would he?

Taking a deep breath, she picked up. "H-hello?"

"Laney, it's Noah. You sound shaky."

Laney sank onto her couch. "It's terrible being afraid to find out who's on the other end of a phone call. Briana and I are doing fine. I just put her to bed after a dull evening. No indication of anything out of the ordinary." She injected all the lightness she could muster into her words. If only he were sitting here in her living room, she might feel some of it. What a pitiful creature she was to pine after someone who saw only another staff member.

"Have you called your parents yet?"

"That's next on the agenda."

"Well, then, I'd better let you get to it. I'm here if you need anything."

A picture of him holding her appeared in her mind's eye, but she squelched it. "Thanks. I appreciate all you've done."

"You're welcome. Hang in there."

The line went dead, and Laney cradled the

receiver in her hand. She dreaded the next conversation as much as she needed it. Her parents would be devastated that the nightmare had returned. Too bad they'd moved away from St. Cloud, Minnesota, a few months ago for Dad to take a high-paying job as a vice president for a big corporation. Laney punched in their Louisville, Kentucky, number.

The phone had scarcely begun to ring when a familiar voice said hello.

"Hi, Mom, it's me."

"Oh, sweetie, we were about to call *you*."

The tears in her mother's voice told Laney she wasn't first with the news to her parents. "I suppose you've heard from *Supervisory Special Agent* Justin Burns."

"We just got off the phone with him." Her dad's voice came from another extension. "He said you received a threat."

"If you call finding Gracie's backpack on the school playground after recess a threat, then yes. I took it that way."

"Does the little Bree-bee know?" His voice dripped concern.

"I could hardly keep it from her. The whole town is in an uproar. Principal Ryder put the entire school on alert and sent informative letters home with the kids for their parents."

"Sounds like your principal knew what to do," her mother put in. "How's Briana taking the news?

Maybe we shouldn't have decided not to tell her about Grace. Look what's—"

"Loretta, there's no use second-guessing ourselves now." Her father's voice took command. "We agreed it was best she not be told until she was older. How could we know this maniac would force our hands?"

"Mom, Dad, don't worry about it," Lainie said. "If anything, Bree is calmer than I am. She's convinced God is guarding us, and Noah Ryder's his helper. I wish I had half her confidence." A sour laugh spurted between her lips.

"Honey, you have more faith than you think," her mother said. "You wouldn't be the strong woman, wonderful mom and terrific teacher you are without it."

The affirmation tasted like a soothing tonic. "Thanks, Mom. I needed that."

"You're welcome."

"Still, it might not be a bad idea for me to hire you a bodyguard," her dad put in.

Laney snickered. "Can you see me wandering around this little burg with some goon in my shadow? Briana and I are conspicuous enough as it is. So let's talk about something else. Did Agent Burns indicate if they have any good leads?"

Her dad snorted. "Since when does that man indicate anything? He dictates and he interrogates."

"Sounds like you talked to the same Burns I did."

Laney's chuckle joined with her parents', but an ache in her throat followed. "I miss Gracie. I'd forgotten how cute and funny she could be. Then today, all this turmoil dredged up a whole bunch of Grace pictures in my mind. Like the way she'd scrunch up her nose and cross her eyes, Mom, when you served something for supper she didn't like. Or how she'd sit in your lap, Dad, and kiss your cheek over and over for no reason at all."

Her mother sniffled. "Do you remember how she'd follow you around so close, Laney? You'd practically trip over her every time you turned around."

Laney's heart turned to lead. She hated it now that she'd resented it then. "I remember." The confession scraped against her voice box.

A half hour of tears and recollections later, the call ended, and Laney flopped her head back against the couch, utterly drained. If only she could go straight to bed. Hibernating until the monster who stole Gracie was caught sounded like a splendid plan. In her dreams. She forced herself off the soft cushions and took a seat in front of the computer desk on the other side of the living room. One more mission to accomplish before she called it a day.

While the computer booted up, she got a glass of apple juice from the kitchen. The phone rang again, and she picked it up without thought. It was a television news reporter asking for an interview. Laney politely but firmly declined.

Then she settled in front of the monitor. Her fingers danced across the keys. She'd run a search on Noah Ryder. There had to be something significant to know about him besides the scuttlebutt that he'd attended Southwest Minnesota State University in Marshall, Minnesota, for his teaching degree. Time for a different approach.

The search engine came up, and Laney typed in Noah Ryder. She discovered he had a Facebook account like she did. Would it be forward of her to submit a friend request to him, so their profile pages were accessible to each other? She decided against it for the moment.

She continued searching under Noah Ryder, but learned nothing she didn't already know. A few other Noah Ryders came up that couldn't possibly be him—wrong age, location, etc. Laney smothered a yawn. She should hit the sack. Yet the innuendos about Noah from Sheriff Lindoll and Agent Burns wouldn't leave her alone.

She typed in a search under Ryder. The more general search would generate a vast array of hits, but she was going to check every one until she found something more about her enigmatic boss. This was desperate times.

A couple of pages of listings were connected to the moving company by that name. Then there were a few hits about a Ryder family tree, but these never mentioned a Noah on one of the branches. Finally, many pages into the search results, an intriguing article caught her eye—Investigator Unites Mother and Son After Dangerous Manhunt.

Laney clicked on the link and started reading, then slumped. The investigator mentioned in the headline was *Franklin* Ryder, not Noah. She read on anyway. The article involved a missing child. Not that an abusive husband and father snatching his son from the custodial mother was a new tale these days, but it sounded as if this dad was a devious piece of work who eluded law enforcement time after time…until Franklin Ryder, Private Investigator, took the case. In the photo that accompanied the article, a pretty young woman beamed for the camera as she cuddled a chubby, dark-haired boy.

"Nuts!" Laney exclaimed. She'd hoped for a picture of this whiz-bang investigator. She peered at the photo. Someone was walking away in the background. It was a side shot too grainy to identify the person, but there was something familiar about the stride and the confident set of the shoulders. And the man was a blond, like Noah.

Heart trip-hammering, Laney plugged in a search for Franklin Ryder. Page after page of articles came up. She had her confirmation on the first one. The man she knew as Principal Noah Ryder stared back at her from the screen.

Headache and exhaustion forgotten, Laney spent until the wee hours devouring news articles about Franklin Ryder. There were even videos. But news reports on the man abruptly ceased six years ago. Why had he suddenly given up investigating? And why change his name? Wasn't he proud of his work that restored the lost to their families, or at least got them justice and closure?

The media dubbed him a "relentless bloodhound" and "a kidnapper's worst nightmare." Excitement squeezed Laney's chest as she continued reading stories and quotes from people who saw him in action. "It's downright eerie the way Ryder can put himself inside the skin of a kidnapper and figure out what he's going to do almost before he does it," said a law officer involved in one of the cases.

Why hide from a reputation like that? If the cops weren't delivering on a missing persons case, Franklin Ryder was the guy to hire, especially if the victim was a child. Franklin was passionate about kids, just like the Noah that Laney knew. There was way more to Principal Ryder than anyone in this town had a clue about, except maybe for Sheriff Lindoll. The man's remarks and reactions today suddenly made perfect sense. And somewhere along the trail of Noah's career as an investigator, he and Agent Burns had clearly locked horns.

Finally, Laney rose and stretched, but she wore a smile on her face. Hope had gained ascendancy over fear. She'd found an answer that couldn't be more clearly from God if He'd etched the message on her forehead.

Whatever it took, whatever it cost, she was going to hire Noah/Franklin Ryder to find the monster that killed Gracie and threatened Briana.

Well before time for school to start, Noah sat in his office on Friday morning going over his notes about yesterday's incident. Why did he write these things down anyway? And why couldn't he put the notes away and concentrate on school business? Old habits died hard, but then, he was responsible for the safety of everyone in this school. As long as he kept that motive in the forefront, he'd be all right.

A rap sounded on his door. "It's open," he called. Probably Miss Aggie, miffed to discover he'd arrived ahead of her. But his visitor was most decidedly not his angular administrative assistant. The slender female in form-fitting jeans and a tailored aqua blouse walked toward his desk, and his mouth went dry. "Laney? What are you doing here?"

"I'm a desperate woman in need of your expertise." She laid a small stack of news reports printed off the Internet in front of him.

Noah's heart leaped against his ribs. He kept his gaze averted as he forced his composure back into place. Finally, he allowed himself to look up. Laney's pleading blue eyes clawed at his resolve. He pushed the papers back toward her. "What's all this about?"

Her nostrils flared. "I called Sheriff Lindoll this morning and asked him about these."

Noah groaned and scrubbed a hand over his face.

"Here's what he said," she continued. "I quote. 'I'm not going to deny your research, Ms. Thompson. If it is him, it'd be great to have someone in on the action who can tweak those federal guys' noses.'" She planted her palms on his desk and leaned toward him, bringing their faces inches apart. "You can tweak noses or cut them off for all I care, as long as you catch a child killer. I can pay you whatever you want…or my dad can, at least."

Noah leaned back in his chair, gaining distance. "I can't do that anymore." Each word came out clipped and razor-thin.

Laney drew herself up tall. "Your real name is Franklin Ryder. You're an ace investigator. What do you mean you can't do what you're so great at doing?"

He shook his head. "My real name is Noah Franklin Ryder, Jr. To differentiate between me and my dad, I grew up being called Franklin. By the time I quit the P.I. business my dad had passed on, so I reverted to Noah and embarked on a new career. I love being a school principal, and I meant what I said. I can't go back to what I did before."

"Can't or won't."

"Both."

Something deflated in the woman before him, and the sight cut deep. She sank into a chair. "Why not?"

"I'm not too proud to admit that I'm washed up as an investigator." He frowned and studied his desktop, pain surging through him. "Something happened half a dozen years back."

"When the news articles about you ceased."

"That'd be the time. Look," he squared his gaze with hers, "I won't go into detail, but the wheels came off on an investigation and an innocent person died."

"Was it your fault?"

"I ask myself that every day."

A wounded laugh bubbled from her throat. "Join the club. I ask myself the same thing about Gracie."

Noah leaned his elbows on his desk and studied the woman before him. "Why would her death be your fault?"

Her gaze fell away. "I was the big sister, the protector. I was supposed to walk Gracie all the way home from school that day. Instead, I went as far as our home block, then I ran off with my friends to play. I figured she could make it the rest of the way by herself. I was wrong." She lifted her head, cheeks whitewashed. "It was my birthday. I wanted to have some fun, and my *fun* cost my sister her life. What a selfish little fool!"

"Aw, Laney." Noah reached a hand across the desk, though it couldn't reach far enough to touch her. "You have no idea how many times I've heard stories like that from family members looking for someone to blame. Quite often themselves. One moment of common carelessness ends in tragedy, and people can't forgive themselves for being human. You were just a kid being a kid."

Laney's hard expression shattered, and she sobbed. "I hope…" she hiccupped "…one day…I can believe that." Tears made twin tracks down her cheeks.

Blinking away the sting behind his eyes, Noah grabbed a tissue from the box on his credenza. He came around his desk and handed it to her. She took the tissue and scrubbed as if she would wipe away memories.

"I hope you take those words to heart. They're true." Noah laid a hand on her shoulder. "Hard-won truths like that are the best I can offer. Please keep your knowledge about my former business name and occupation to yourself. Investigating is not in me anymore."

She stared up at him. "You're wrong. A gift like that doesn't just go away. If you can lie to yourself so completely, how can I be sure you're not telling me a pretty story, too?" She shrugged off his hand, then rose like a grand diva and stalked from the room.

Noah watched her leave, every thought frozen in his brain. A few moments later, he shook himself. Her statement was ridiculous. He wasn't lying about being washed up. She didn't know what she was talking about. How could she? She wasn't there when it all went down.

The sound of drawers opening and closing in the outer office signaled that Miss Aggie had arrived. Had she encountered the irate Laney Thompson? Noah stepped into the reception area. One look at his secretary's face told him what he needed to know.

"You *are* going to help that poor girl?" Miss Aggie pronounced.

"But—"

"No excuses, young man." She shook a finger at him and turned away.

Noah retreated into his sanctuary. What did Miss Aggie know about him? How did she find out? The same way Laney did?

He plopped down behind his desk and put his head in his hands. *Lord, how can I take the chance again?* But how could he live with himself if something bad happened to either Laney or Briana because he didn't get involved? He slumped against his chair and tilted his head back, scrubbing his cheeks with his palms. Then again, how could he survive if he *did* take the case, and the worst happened anyway?

The miserable morning passed like an ant crawling across hot coals. Most of those coals were hidden behind Miss Aggie's silent stares. Near noon, he escaped to help supervise the early recess.

Some of the adult workers seemed subdued after yesterday, but if anything, the children were more boisterous and active. Noah kept busy making sure they used the equipment safely and respected each other's boundaries, but he didn't forget to push the swings and give rides on the merry-go-round.

Laughing, Noah drifted toward the fence to take a break and observe the whole playground. A figure in his peripheral vision caught his attention. He turned his head and froze.

A short, burly man in a business suit stood in a shadowed spot near the fence. Hands fisting and flexing, his gaze devoured one specific cluster of giggling little girls.

FOUR

Noah spoke a few words to one of the aides on the playground. She hurried toward the building to call the police. A fast walk took Noah to one of the openings in the fence about fifty feet from the man in the suit. He kept the corner of his eye on the intruder, but was careful not to stare in a way that might draw attention. If this louse was up to no good, the smallest hint that he'd been spotted would send him scuttling away. The man's focus never wavered from the children. Noah's lips thinned. Maybe his caution was wasted on the pervert.

Reaching the street, he circled behind the guy. He needed to catch him by surprise. His pulse thundered in his ears, and the burn on his face didn't come from the sun. The muscles in his arms and legs tensed like piano wires. *Patience. Remember? That's how it's done.* His fists would rather make pulp out of a sicko like this than hold him for the police, but that's what he'd do, law-abiding civilian that he was.

Just a little bit closer. Almost there. His breathing sounded way too loud in his own ears.

The guy ran a hand across a bald spot on the back of his head and then turned from the fence. His eyes widened to find Noah almost upon him.

"Hold it! We need to talk," Noah said.

The man yelped and whirled away. Noah charged and his fingers closed on the back of the man's suit jacket. The intruder jerked the smooth fabric out of Noah's grasp as he took off up the sidewalk at a sprint. Surprisingly quick for his squat stature, he gained a few strides. Then Noah ducked his head and put his own sprint into gear.

The man darted onto the street, heading for a blue Impala parked and running at the curb a short way up the street. *Oh, no, you don't!* Their feet thundered in near unison across the pavement. Noah lunged forward and rammed into the stalker as they reached the rear of the car. The stocky guy was more flab than muscle, and Noah's shoulder buried itself in the man's back. Breath exploded from the guy's gut, and they fell across the rear end of the Chevy. The acrid stench of car exhaust bit Noah's nostrils as he struggled to control the flailing man.

"I…didn't do…anything!" The stalker's voice came out in hoarse pants.

"Strangers…staring at…little kids…don't sit well with me." Noah finally wrestled the guy to the pavement and clamped his wrists together while he pressed his knee into the small of the man's back.

The sudden bleep of a siren announced the arrival of a city black and white that pulled up beside the Impala. Deputy David Carlson climbed out.

"What have you got here?" The officer hustled toward them, then stopped short. "Eddie Foreman!"

The man beneath Noah quit wiggling. "You know this guy?" Noah stared up at the deputy.

"Me and Ed went to school together. He moved to Watertown, South Dakota, about an hour from here, but he's okay."

Noah glared down at his captive. Just because a local police officer was acquainted with the suspect didn't mean he wasn't guilty. But the man wasn't likely to run again with both a cop and a principal breathing down his neck. Noah released Eddie's arms, stood up and backed away a marginal step.

The stalker struggled to his feet, huffing, face apple-red. He adjusted his suit jacket. "I told you I wasn't doing anything."

"Now, Ed," Carlson crossed his arms, "lurking around school yards is frowned upon, even in Cottonwood Grove."

Ed's gaze fell to loafers that had seen better days. "You knew Bonnie and I split?"

"You don't say!" The officer's arms fell to his sides.

Noah stared from one man to the other. What was this? Old home week?

"Yeah." Ed lifted his eyes. Sad, all right, just like

Briana described. "She got custody of Becca and moved back to the old hometown. I was just—" A soft sob left the man's barrel chest, and he rubbed a pudgy hand across his face. "I deliver office supplies around here, and then I stop at noon to catch a glimpse of my girl. That's all." He sent a glare toward Noah.

Carlson's face pinched. "Sure am sorry, but you'd best not be hanging around the school grounds without permission."

"I understand." The other man nodded. "I'll go now." He shuffled toward his car door.

"Hey, wait. You can't—" Noah started, but the officer lifted a palm. He clamped his lips shut against angry words. This guy was not cleared of anything in his books.

"Ed, you follow me to the station and give a statement first." Barnes jerked his head in the direction of the courthouse. "Some folks down there are going to have questions for you."

"You mean in case I want to press charges for assault?" Ed sneered toward Noah.

"You might have a case if I'd done half what I wanted," Noah said.

The lurker paled.

Carlson wagged his head. "Nobody's going to press charges, unless you can't give satisfactory answers, Ed. Then it's you who could be in a world of trouble."

Deflated, the man got in his car, and both

vehicles drove away. Noah watched them with his hands on his hips. Hank would make sure Ed could account for every minute of his time yesterday. He'd know that there was a reason Becca's mother got full custody of the little girl.

Would he turn out to be the slimy rodent who left that backpack on the playground for Laney to find?

"Every member on the staff is primed to keep an eye on Briana," Ellen Kline told Laney on Monday outside Briana's classroom after she dropped her daughter off.

Gnawing her lower lip, Laney watched through the doorway as Briana took her seat and started laughing and chatting with her neighbor. How could the little girl stay so carefree? But then, did she really want her child to be full of fear?

Laney let out a breath. "Thanks, Ellen. I know she's in good hands."

"You go and let yourself focus on your students." Ellen patted Laney's arm.

"I'll give it my best shot." With a wave toward her friend, she headed for her room.

En route, she passed Richard Hodge striding in the other direction with a wrench in his hand. His dark gaze brooded on her, and she shivered. No one complained about the man's work, and he never caused trouble—other than creeping her out with his dark looks.

She halted and stared at his retreating back. If

attitude and opportunity meant anything, he'd be a candidate for the one who left that backpack on the playground. Was she looking at Gracie's killer? Her stomach twisted. He would have been a teenager at the time, but teens could do awful things. Did an angry adolescent commit a horrible act and grow up into this moody, depressed man? Maybe she should mention the possibility to Noah.

Where had that thought come from? She marched toward her classroom. Principal Ryder had made it clear he wasn't taking the case.

In her room, she began organizing the day's material, but her thoughts weren't on her lesson plans. All weekend, she'd worked on forgiving Noah for his refusal to help. Good thing he hadn't tried to contact her on Saturday or Sunday—the chicken!—or she might have given him a piece of her mind.

A happy hum of giggles and childish shouts and clattering locker doors carried to Laney's ears. Town kids trickling in. It was too early for the buses to have arrived. One of her students wandered through her door to collect his morning hug. The child then left for his regular classroom. As much as possible, the special needs children were mainstreamed, and she saw them in groups or singly on a specific schedule each day.

About fifteen minutes before school was due to start, the noise outside her door increased exponentially. The buses had dumped their loads. She could expect a few more visitors before class went into session. Soon first grader Mathilda Stier, a high-functioning Down's child, stepped through her door. She barely crept toward Laney's desk, cradling a shoebox tied with string as if it contained eggs.

What had she thought to bring her? Her students were always dropping off little gifts. Last week it had been a sparkly rock from Gordon, and the week before that Sheree thought she'd love a goose feather from her family's farm. Maybe the box really did contain a bird's nest of eggs.

"What have you got there, Mattie?" Laney asked.

The little girl beamed her pleasant, vague smile and held out the box. "For you, Miss Thompson. It's a pweasant."

"Thank you, sweetheart." She took the offering. It wasn't light enough to be feathers or heavy enough to be rocks. "I wonder what it could be."

Mathilda shrugged her small shoulders. Still smiling, she left.

Grinning, Laney studied the string. It ran around the short side of the box, then looped on the bottom to come up again the long way and tie in a knot on top. Mathilda hadn't done this. Velcro was her thing. Her mother must have helped. Laney took her scissors from her desk drawer and snipped the string. She flipped the cover off the box, and her smile iced over.

She fought for breath, but her lungs thought all

the oxygen had been sucked from the room. The glassy gaze of a china doll stared back at her in a mockery of what had once been beauty. A lightning-bolt crack ran from skull to chin, and the delicate features were smeared with something bright red. A lock of blond hair at the temple was clasped in a blue plastic barette. Laney recognized the item.

Grace had been wearing it the day she disappeared.

FIVE

"No, Mattie. You're not in trouble." From a seat beside the little girl at a student table in her classroom, Laney patted the child's pudgy hand. "You did the right thing bringing the box to me."

Across the table from them, Noah nodded and smiled for Mathilda's benefit. His head still reeled from the horrifying object Laney had brought to him minutes ago. They'd left the box and its grisly contents locked in his office while they interviewed the child. The little girl wriggled under their scrutiny. The tension that filled both adults must have transmitted to her.

He sat forward. "We'd like to know who gave it to you, what the person said, and when and where they gave it to you."

The child reddened and her mouth worked like a fish, but nothing came out.

Laney scrunched her cute nose at him. "Four questions in one." She returned her attention to her student. "Let's start with who gave you the box, Mattie. Can you tell us that?"

The little girl bobbed her head, and shadows dispelled from the full moon face. Noah settled back to watch the master at work. She knew how to handle kids, especially the more challenged ones.

"Who was it?" Laney prompted.

"The mailman," the little girl announced as if sharing the day of the week with simple folks.

"The mail—" Noah burst out, then stifled himself at Laney's upraised palm. *Don't get ahead of things here, buddy.*

"What made you think it was the mail carrier?" She leaned closer to the child.

"The stripey pants. And the shirt was blue, too. That's what the mailman wears."

"Good observation." Laney smiled at the girl, who grinned back. "Where were you when this mailman gave you the package?"

"By our mailbox at the end of our driveway."

"While you were waiting for the bus?"

The little head bobbed again.

"Have you ever seen this particular mailman before?"

Mathilda nodded, and electric tension coursed through Noah. Maybe they'd get a name, or at least a lead on a specific person.

"I see the man in the stripey pants every day I'm not in school," the child said. "'Cept a course on Sunday."

Noah suppressed a groan. Like most witnesses, Mathilda made an assumption based on a visual association—that all men in blue uniforms with stripes down the legs of the pants are mailmen—and didn't bother to notice the face above the clothing. Or maybe in Mathilda's situation, she wasn't capable of more differentiation. Noah's palms fisted. This creep sure knew how to play his camouflage. And taking advantage of a mentally handicapped child was scraping the bottom of the barrel. Correction, this guy was scraping the fungus *below* the barrel—and worse, considering what he'd done to Laney's sister.

And might do again.

If someone didn't stop him.

He frowned and crossed his arms. Not going there. Plenty of capable lawmen were on the case. Even Burns had a rep for making good collars. Noah would admit that much. And Hank was topnotch, small town or not. That's what he'd kept telling himself over the weekend when his hand hovered over the telephone, itching to make a call to Laney. She'd never know how much anguish such self-control cost him when he wanted to wrap her and Briana in a cocoon and carry them away to a safe place. But where was that in this world?

Laney sent him a long look, as if wondering where his head had gone. He sat up straighter and nodded.

She turned toward her student. "The postman

doesn't usually come to your place before school, does he?"

Mathilda gazed down at the table, where her hands rested, stubby fingers flexing. "He said it was a special delivery for my pretty teacher, and he was going to let me give it to you 'cuz I'm special, too." She lifted her head, and devotion glowed toward Laney from small brown eyes.

"You are special, Mattie," Laney affirmed. "Did the man say anything else?"

The child scratched an ear beneath dark hair. "Only my teacher could open it. And I was real, real careful. Didn't let nobody else touch the box. Uh-uh!" Mathilda swung her head back and forth.

"Excellent," Noah said. At least, if no one handled the container except Mathilda and Laney forensic evidence might be less tainted. "Is there anything else you remember about this man?"

Mathilda scrunched up her thick eyebrows. "His dog must of got one of his shoes."

"His dog?" Laney tucked in her chin. "Did he have an animal with him?"

"Naw." The child shook her head. "But one of the toes was coming apart. Like when our dog got my brother's shoe." She giggled.

Noah lifted his feet. "Which shoe was it? Do you remember?"

"That one." The child pointed to his left loafer.

"And the other shoe was fine?" He withdrew his feet.

"Yup. All good."

Noah frowned. Both of Eddie's shoes had been scuffed up.

"But he had clown hands," the little girl added.

Laney's wide-eyed gaze met Noah's. "Clown hands! What do you mean, honey?" She touched the little girl's arm.

"Like at the circus. All white and funny and not—" She crossed her eyes as if searching inside for the right word. "Not real. You know!" Frustration tinged the child's voice.

"The mailman was wearing gloves?" Noah canted his head.

A smile spread across the little girl's face. "No, silly. It's not winter time." She fluttered her fingers. "They felt like my bouncy ball."

"He touched you?" Horror bled from Laney's tone.

Mathilda shrank in her seat. "Right here." She patted her left cheek. "When he handed me the box."

An audible breath left Laney's mouth. "That's okay, then." She cleared her throat, darting a glance at Noah, who didn't trust himself to utter a word. "You did great, Mattie. Thanks so much." But every tense plane of her face proclaimed that nothing was all right. "I'll have an aide take you back to your classroom."

"Okay." The little girl hopped up. The poor kid was probably very ready to get away from the grilling.

Laney rose and took her student by the hand, but her gaze was distant and haunted.

The little girl looked up at her teacher. "Was it nice?"

"What?" Laney focused on her charge.

"Your present."

"It was…a doll." The words came out a bit ragged.

Mathilda nodded as they reached the door. "That's good. I like dollies."

Laney let Mathilda out and exchanged a few murmured words with someone in the hall, then wheeled toward Noah.

"Surgical gloves," he said.

"On his hands?"

"Yes. Mathilda has probably never seen any and didn't know how to describe them." He scowled. This perp was smart and devious and ruthless. Fat chance they'd find any of his prints on the box.

Laney approached the table. The drawn and frightened look on her face wrapped fingers of guilt around his heart.

"We'll have to take the next step now." His tone edged toward a growl.

"Call the sheriff and the feds?" Laney wilted into her chair. "Burns is going to have a fit that we didn't call him *before* we talked to Mattie."

"Tough cookies." Noah rose. "I'll go do the deed."

A wild giggle spurted from her throat. "Is it a crime to impersonate a federal employee like a mailman?"

Noah snorted. "That'll be the least of his worries when I get my hands on him." He stalked from the room.

Finally alone in her room after the interrogations, Laney sat slumped at her desk. She glanced at the clock, then rubbed her forehead. Three horrible hours had passed, and the lower grades would be at lunch right now, including her Briana. Thank goodness, her little girl hadn't been involved in this round of questioning. Just poor little Mathilda and her mother and father.

Laney had called the child's parents in while Noah notified Hank. She'd warned Mr. and Mrs. Stier to come loaded for bear when talking to Agent Burns, but still the child had come out in tears and the parents pale and shell-shocked. It was all Laney could do not to slap the smug look off Agent Burns's face as he followed them out of the interview room. Then Noah had dismissed Mathilda for the day and escorted the troubled family from the building. He hadn't said anything to her then, and she hadn't seen him since.

What had Noah meant by that last statement in her classroom, before he made the phone call that started the flood of lawmen in the school all over again? He'd talked as if he was going after this creep. Had he reconsidered? Was he going to take her case, or was he only speaking as an angry school principal?

"Laney, can I talk to you?" Noah's voice called from her doorway.

She looked up and motioned him inside.

He perched on the edge of her desk, mouth down-turned. "The Stiers have decided to keep their daughter home until the perp is caught."

Laney shook her head. "I don't blame them. The poor child has had a scare that will rattle her world. She'll probably be afraid of mailmen from now on."

"At least she's not missing…or worse."

She gulped and fought prickles behind her eyes. This man had approached Mathilda so easily in a guise that the little girl trusted. What if he found a simple way to get to Briana?

"The parents told me everything Burns wrung out of their daughter," Noah continued. "Most of it was the same as she told us, but there were a few additional details. Evidently, the bogus mailman wore sunglasses and a hat, and his hair was the color of straw."

Laney snorted. "What are the odds he was wearing a wig?"

"Excellent, I'd say." He folded his hands in his lap. "I've given it a lot of thought this morning, and I believe you and your daughter should also end your school year today."

Laney's gaze fell to the cheerful disarray of colored papers, craft items and lesson plans on her desktop. "What about my students?"

"There's only four days left of the school year. They can handle mainstream for that long. Fill out your student evaluations at home, and I'll make sure Briana gets to finish any tests or assignments from your apartment. She'll be passed on to the next grade. No problem."

She quavered a sigh. "I agree with the wisdom of your decision for the safety of the school, but it hurts."

"For your safety and peace of mind, too, Laney. You can be with your daughter every minute. The FBI will have you under surveillance, along with every law enforcement officer in town. And I'll check up on you, too."

Her pulse leaped. Would he really? Her nostrils pinched and she glanced away. A phone call or two didn't mean much if an old wound kept him from doing what truly mattered—catching the scum that threatened her daughter.

"So how long are Burns and his bunch going to stick around?" She twiddled a paper clip between her fingers. "The FBI won't waste manpower on staking out my place forever if they don't see some action. And so far, our lurking creep has run below everybody's radar."

Noah nodded. "I agree we're dealing with a clever, subtle stalker, but he seems to be obsessed with taunting you. So maybe he'll dance too close to the flame and get caught."

"I'm sure that's what the FBI is hoping for. I feel like the worm on the end of a hook." Laney brushed strands of hair off her forehead. "I'd better get my things together so I can leave." She rose, grabbed up a sheaf of papers and hugged them to her chest.

Tears pressed against the backs of her eyes. After receiving the doll, she'd run instinctively to Noah. But he was leaving her and Briana in the hands of an FBI supervisor who regarded them as little more than bait, and a small-town police force that didn't often deal with anything more serious than vandalism and penny-ante drug dealing.

And then there was her career to consider. She gazed around her room. Was she leaving this school forever?

Noah stood, and she looked him in the eye. "Maybe it's a selfish thing to be concerned about at a time like this, but I'm nervous about my position here. I don't have tenure yet. With the danger that's been visited on the students because of me, the school board may think twice about renewing my contract."

"You know that's not my decision to make." His words were gentle.

"But your recommendation makes a big difference."

One side of his firm mouth lifted. "I admire your gift with the students. I won't have a problem recommending you in the professional arena. But I agree that the school board may not consider you a good risk if this joker hasn't been caught before next fall." He rubbed the side of one finger across his upper lip. Then he lifted his head. The set of his mouth betrayed an abiding pain, but his gaze held determination. "That's one of the many reasons I can't dodge my conscience any longer. I've decided to take your case."

Laney dropped the papers. They fluttered to the floor as she gave a glad cry and flung her arms around Noah's neck.

For the briefest instant, Noah returned the hug, then he set her away from him.

She backed off, cheeks hot. "I guess you can see how much your involvement means to me."

He'd better not think she meant anything else by that hug. Sure, she was interested in him as a man, but romance had been the farthest thing from her mind right then. Hadn't it? Pleasant tingles said maybe her subconscious had a mind of its own.

He lifted a hand in farewell. "I'll stop by your apartment this evening, and we can strategize. You can fill me in on the details of what happened with your sister."

Laney nodded. Talking about her sister's disappearance would hurt like lancing an abscess, but it was necessary. "Come about seven-thirty. You can say good-night to Briana and then we can talk."

After Noah left, she straightened her room and

stuffed everything she thought she might need into a tote bag, then went to collect her daughter. The memory of Noah's arms around her replayed in her mind over and over. If only he'd held her a few seconds longer. In that breathless moment, she'd tasted a feeling she hadn't enjoyed since tragedy marred her childhood—a sense of safety.

SIX

Noah stood outside Laney's apartment door at 7:29 p.m. He knew the exact minute because he'd checked his watch a half dozen times while walking up three flights of stairs. He didn't want to arrive early and betray how eager he was to be with Laney and her cute-as-a-button little girl. Then again, he didn't want to be late. That would be disrespectful to her situation. Noah knocked on the door. A few seconds later, locks rattled and the door opened to reveal Laney wearing a shy smile.

"You're very prompt," she said.

Warmth crept up Noah's neck. Maybe all his planning had succeeded only in painting himself a bit obsessive.

"Hi, Mr. Ryder," chirped the little girl by Laney's side.

Noah bent over with his hands on his knees. "Hi, there, princess."

Briana giggled. "You noticed my pajamas."

In truth, he hadn't, but as she skipped away, he

saw that her pink pjs were adorned with ball-gowned princesses.

"Come on," she called. "We're going to play Chutes and Ladders."

Laney wrinkled her nose. "I hope you don't mind. She's had her heart set on a game with you all evening. When that's done, I'll put her to bed."

Chuckling, Noah entered the apartment. He found himself in a neat living room furnished with a couch, a couple of stuffed chairs and a modest-size, flat screen TV. The décor was tastefully simple in a country theme.

He turned toward his hostess. "I warn you, I'm downright dangerous at Chutes and Ladders."

"I'm very afraid." She laughed, motioning him into a small, neat kitchen. The game was set up on the table, and Briana was already perched on a chair.

"You sit there, Mr. Ryder." The little girl pointed to a chair on her right. "And Mama there." She pointed to the opposite seat. "And I get to go first."

"Of course." Noah slid into his assigned place. "Princesses always go first."

The little girl's blue eyes danced, and Laney sent him a look he'd trade an arm and a leg to keep on seeing. A half hour later, after the princess triumphed at the game and was put to bed, Laney brought a cup of coffee to him where he sat in one of the stuffed chairs in her living room.

She eased onto the end of the couch closest to

his chair, cradling her mug. "I suppose we need to get down to business. First of all, I'd like to assure you that I've spoken to my dad, and he's more than glad to pay whatever your rate is."

Noah suppressed a sigh. He hated to start in with this bad business again. But then, that's why he was here. "Don't give my fee a thought at this point." He took a drink from his mug. She made good coffee. "I'll hammer that out with your father at an appropriate moment."

Laney nodded. "Fair enough. I suppose my part is to answer your questions. What would you like to know?"

"First of all, I'd like to be as assured as I possibly can of Briana's safety."

"I'm with you on that." Laney sipped her brew.

"Getting her out of here might be the best option. Is her father around? Maybe he could take her."

She snickered and shook her head. "I have no idea where Clayton is. We haven't seen him since Briana was two months old."

"I'm sorry." Was he really? The little leap of glee in his gut said no. He hid his reaction by focusing on another swallow from his cup.

"It's for the best, really." She set her mug on a trivet on the side table. "Clay and I were frivolous college kids when we met, fresh out of high school. We fell madly in love—or so we thought—and pretty soon Briana was on the way. She wasn't in our plans, but I couldn't think of her as a mistake. Clay did." She scowled. "Marrying me was his attempt at honor, I suppose, but he bailed after two months of being trapped in the trials of infant care. End of story."

"His loss." Noah crossed an ankle over his knee. *And some other lucky man's gain.* He kept that part to himself.

Laney blushed and glanced away. "The only place I could send Bree that I'd feel comfortable is my parents' home in Louisville, Kentucky."

Noah nodded. "I think you should both go."

"Both? But I want to help you with the investigation."

He frowned, evil memories crowding his head about that other time his client got involved. "The best thing you can do is find a safe hidey-hole and let me figure out who this guy is."

"Without distractions." Her gaze was frank and direct, not offended.

He answered with a thin smile. The lady was sharp and level-headed.

She frowned but nodded. "I suppose I can understand that. I just want this guy caught and put away so I can take a deep breath again."

Noah nodded, a weight leaving his chest. Laney wasn't going to argue. Renee would have given him twenty reasons why she needed to get in on the action, and look what her enthusiasm got her— an early grave. But then, she hadn't had a daughter to think about, and life had taught Laney caution at an early age.

"Tell you what," he said. "You lay low here for the next few days until school is out. You can finish your evaluations and make sure Briana gets her work done." He polished off his coffee and set the mug aside. "I checked with the sheriff, and he's heard sort of sideways from one of the FBI agents in town that the team is heading back to Minneapolis tomorrow. But they're leaving an agent to shadow you around in case this guy tries to make another move."

"Great!" She rolled her eyes. "I get to keep my shadow."

"You don't find that comforting?"

"I don't find comfort in any aspect of this situation." Her nostrils flared. "I don't mean to sound ungrateful, but even the efforts to protect me are intrusive."

Noah looked away and studied a painting of a pastoral scene on the wall. He wasn't about to tell her that, in his opinion, Agent Burns wasn't as concerned about protecting Laney or Briana as he was about adding a major notch in his belt by solving a cold case.

"You said until school lets out." She cocked her head. "What did you have in mind then?"

He smiled. She didn't miss much. "I'll escort you to Louisville personally. I'd like a chance to talk to your parents before I visit the scene of the original crime."

Laney shifted in her seat. "Maybe while we're marking time until the end of the school year, you could do a little research on Richard Hodge."

"The school custodian?"

She nodded. "I don't have any reason to suspect him other than the built-in opportunity he'd have to plant that backpack on the playground, and he doesn't seem to like me."

Noah let out a wry chuckle. "I've yet to determine if Richard likes anyone, including himself. But I've checked people out on less. Sure, I'll look into Richard." He unbent his leg and stretched it out beside the other one. "Maybe you heard that I caught a guy watching the kids on the playground yesterday."

"Ellen told me." She nodded. "Sounds like he was some brokenhearted dad."

"I don't think the story's that simple. Hank told me Edward Foreman claims he was on the road for his office supply business the day the backpack was left on the playground. But following up his story, the sheriff's office can't account for at least two hours of his time. The playground watcher's not off the hook as far as I'm concerned." Noah gave her a quick description of the man. "If you see him anywhere near, call the cops pronto."

"Don't worry, I will." Her brief laugh held a sharp edge. "Anyone else I should know about?"

Noah planted his elbows on his knees. "Do you know a man by the name of Glen Crocker?"

"You mean the electrician? Sure. The building super had him up here to fix an outlet problem a few weeks ago." She gasped. "You mean, he's a suspect?"

"He went missing the day before the backpack appeared and hasn't surfaced since. The timing could be a coincidence, but it's enough to warrant a little digging."

Laney pressed a hand to her cheek. "I've never heard a bad word about him, but I thought he seemed a little too full of himself."

Noah stiffened. "Did he flirt with you?"

"Not really. Just had that 'I'm all it' strut about him." She wrinkled her nose. "Reminded me of Clayton, only I know that Glen's a family man."

Noah's gaze narrowed. "He didn't show extra attention to Briana, did he?"

Her face paled. "Well, he did seem taken with her. Said something about wishing he had a little girl to round out the family."

He frowned and rubbed the arms of the easy chair. That didn't sound good in light of what he'd discovered.

"What aren't you telling me?" Her tone was more of a demand than a question.

"I called in a favor from a friend in a strategic place." His gaze met hers. She needed to know everything he did about this guy. "Turns out Crocker dodged an indictment for statutory rape sixteen years ago by skipping the country until the statute of limitations ran out. I got the word today and told Hank already. With a history of involvement with a minor, our upstanding electrician just went to the top of the sheriff's suspect list. My friend is sending me a packet with the details of the case that never got to court."

Air gusted between her lips. "And this man has lived and worked here for years, just a clean-cut family man." Her tone held an angry edge. "You never know about people, do you?"

"A criminal history isn't conclusive, just suggestive. And, trust us, we'll follow up. Now, tell me about Grace and the day she disappeared."

His heart clenched as pain settled over Laney's fine features.

Laney wound her fingers together. She'd known this moment would come, but that didn't make the subject any easier to talk about.

She closed her eyes. "We lived in the little community of Grand Valley in southeastern Minnesota at the time. Grand Valley is actually smaller than Cottonwood Grove, and everybody knows everybody and pretty much everything about each other."

"A lot like here." Noah's gentle tones carried to her.

She nodded, but didn't open her eyes. "As I told you, I was supposed to walk Gracie home after school, but I ran off to play with friends as soon as we got to our block." She swallowed a knot in her throat. "When I stepped into my house a couple of hours later, the whole neighborhood was searching for her—and me, too, since I was supposed to be with her." She barked an acrid chuckle. "Relief at my appearance was short-lived as everyone, including me, realized Grace was out there somewhere alone. Or worse, with someone who had taken here."

Laney hugged herself. Foul memories gagged her.

She swallowed and steeled herself to continue. "The sheriff came the next day to say blood was found in a ravine outside of town. They'd test to see if it was Grace's, but I think we all knew right then that she was gone. We found out later it was her blood." She heaved a long breath and opened her eyes. Noah's compassionate gaze rested on her. "There's been no trace of my sister again until the backpack."

He nodded. "Grace was wearing the pack when she disappeared, so it follows that the perp needed to return to wherever he put her in order to retrieve it."

"An unmarked grave." Laney hung her head. A dark and unmourned place sweet Gracie would never be if only Laney had been more interested in acting like a big sister rather than indulging her own few minutes of fun.

"I don't think she's in a grave. Something like a tomb maybe."

Laney's head jerked up. "Why do you say that?"

"If that backpack had been buried in dirt, it would have disintegrated to pulp by now. I'd say it must have been left in a spot with good protection from the elements. Are there any caves around Grand Valley?"

"Some near the ravine where the blood was found. But they've been searched multiple times." She spread her hands.

"Then maybe it's time to look again. The killer might have disturbed something or left fresh evidence when he went to get the pack. Or maybe there's a cave around there that only the killer knows about."

"That would mean he'd have to be someone local." Laney gripped the arm of the couch. "No one on our current suspect list lived in Grand Valley back then. And I can't think of a soul from that town who would be capable of such a thing."

Noah shook his head. "Didn't you just say you never know about people?"

"Why would someone who knew her hurt simple, sweet Gracie?" Horror boggled her mind.

"That we don't know yet, but the taunts you're receiving are purposeful. I think the person we're looking for knows you, whether you know them or not."

Shivers cascaded through Laney. "I hope you're wrong. It's hard enough to think about Gracie's death being random. I don't know if I could handle it being personal."

"Did your family have any enemies in Grand Valley?"

"My family?" She stared at Noah. Had the man lost his mind? "My parents were beloved and respected in the community. Deservedly so."

"I'm sure they were." Noah's tone was soothing. "But jealousy is a powerful motive. Maybe someone at your dad's place of work? Someone you wouldn't necessarily be able to identify, but he could?"

She surged to her feet. "Are you saying that someone was jealous of my dad so they killed his daughter?"

"I'm not saying anything." Noah gazed at her askance. "I'm theorizing. Probing for possibilities."

"Okay, I get it." Laney ran a hand through her hair. "I'm just…thrown by this notion that the killer could be someone familiar with our family. All I can tell you is this." She wagged a finger at him. "We Thompsons have no skeletons in our closets. I should know."

Noah didn't reply, but if someone had invented a nonsensical-notion eraser, Laney would have used it to wipe the skeptical look off his face.

SEVEN

The next morning, Noah got out of the shower to hear the phone ringing. Who would be calling this early? A crisis with Laney? Something at the school? He hastily wrapped a towel around his wet body, hustled into the bedroom, and grabbed the extension.

"You're really starting to tick me off, Ryder," a familiar voice growled.

Burns. Had he found out already that Noah had taken Laney's case? How? He hadn't told anyone yet but her, and she wasn't about to go blabbing her business to her favorite FBI agent. "Feel free to tell me what's on your mind, Burns."

"That's Supervisory Special Agent Burns to you, pal."

Noah could answer, *and I'm Principal Ryder to you,* but he wasn't into one-upping. "Are you still in town?"

A beat of silence followed. "On my way back to

headquarters in Minneapolis. But we've got our finger on the pulse back there."

"Never doubted it."

"The sheriff tells me you called in a favor and got some dope on that electrician who's missing. I thought I told you to stay out of the investigation."

So that was it. Of course, Hank would have been obliged to share the information with the federal agents. "Thank you would do fine."

"We'll take it from here, so don't get any big ideas."

"Have at it." Noah used the towel on his dripping hair. "The quicker this perp is caught, the better."

"We're on the same page with that idea, but let the professionals do their job, Ryder, and you stick to minding the kiddies."

"That's my plan," Noah answered.

Just wait until Burns caught wind of how aggressively he intended to play the protective role where Briana and her mother were concerned. The guy would hit the moon, but there'd be nothing he could do about it. Grinning, Noah hung up the phone.

A few minutes after he arrived at work and before the pre-school madhouse got into full swing, he was on the phone to Laney.

"'Lo." Her voice sounded groggy.

Noah mentally smacked himself. Here he'd given her time off, and he wasn't letting her sleep in. "Sorry to wake you up."

"No worries." Her tone came back more alert.

"My body clock has been trying to get me out of the sack for a while now. I keep resisting because I haven't been sleeping well."

"That's understandable. I'll keep this brief, and maybe you can catch a few more z's before the little princess demands your attention." Noah leaned back in his office chair. "I spoke to our friend Burns this morning, and he's on his way back to Minneapolis."

Laney snorted. "Did you tell him that you're on our case?"

Noah laughed. "He was fuming that I'd discovered that stuff about Glen Crocker before his office did, so I didn't say anything to add fuel to the fire. If he contacts you, don't feel the need to confess. Let the guy find out some other way, and let me take the heat."

"Agent Burns doesn't scare me." Her voice went steely. "I'm not a child anymore."

No, indeed, you're not, Lovely Laney. "I noticed how you held your own with him the day he showed up. Just don't invite trouble. Okay?"

"You got it. Say, one more thing." She paused on an audible breath. "Would it be all right for me to come to the school on Friday after class lets out for the year and set my room in order? You know, get it ready for a fresh new school term?" Her words were bright, and the tone held hope, but she had to be wondering if she'd be decorating that same room come fall.

"That's a good idea. You need to come anyway for the teacher bash."

"The what? Oh, yes, Ellen mentioned something about staff bringing in a potluck of treats and getting together after final bell. Do you think they'll want me there after all the bother and danger I've exposed them to? And I'll have to bring Briana along."

Noah's heart melted. How could she think she wouldn't be welcome? He hadn't heard anyone complain about bother or danger. The sentiment was squarely on her side. "Laney, your coworkers will be disappointed if you don't show. And Briana will be the life of the party."

"You got that last one right." Laney laughed.

"Mommeeee!"

The child's call carried to Noah from a distance.

"There she is now," Laney said. "I'll let you go and talk to you later."

"Sure, we'll stay in close touch." Noah cradled the receiver.

Sounds from the outer office reached his ears. Miss Aggie had arrived. He went to the door and poked his head out. "Good morning."

His cheerful greeting earned an assessing stare. "You're here early again this morning."

He shrugged. "I had some things to take care of."

Miss Aggie humphed. "Wouldn't have anything to do with the one teacher who will be absent today?"

"As a matter of fact," he offered her a sly grin, "I took her case." His staid assistant let out a whoop. "I'll take that as approval."

She sent him a mock scowl. "It's about time you came to your senses, young man."

He leaned a shoulder against the doorframe. "How did you know about me?"

"Remember the Bobby Gray case—little boy you restored to his mother from a deadbeat father?"

Noah nodded. That case had been one of the good ones with a happy ending.

A tiny grin stole across Miss Aggie's lined face. "Bobby's my great-nephew. I knew who you were the day you showed up to interview with the school board, but I kept my yapper shut. Figured if you wanted folks to know, you'd speak up. Since you've taken Laney's case, soon the whole countryside will know, so you can quit stressing and get down to business."

"You're a peach, Miss Aggie." Noah chuckled at the high color that stole across the older woman's cheeks. "And speaking of business, I plan to escort Laney and Briana to her folks' home in Louisville, Kentucky, the day after school closes. Would you be willing to handle those couple of weeks of post-school-year shutdown if I leave it in your capable hands?"

The woman drew herself to military attention. "If thirty years of working in this office means anything, I could pull it off with my eyes closed."

"And one hand tied behind your back, no doubt." He returned to his desk, laughing.

Now if he could just get through these next few days without seeing Laney's lithe form and smiling face in the hallways.

Well before she reached the cafeteria, Laney could hear the sound of adult laughter and voices of the staff celebrating the end of another school year. Briana skipped up the hallway ahead of her. Laney restrained the impulse to call her daughter back, so she could hold her hand when they entered the party. Would everyone stop talking and stare at them? After Gracie went missing, she'd experienced that reaction from people too many times. Her stomach tightened. How she hated reliving all these little experiences that she'd tried to forget.

Laney accelerated her pace and caught up with her daughter, who sent her a bright smile. Briana did love parties, and she was never intimidated by a room full of adults. It would be nice if Laney could say the same. They neared the door, and she inhaled a lungful of oxygen. Might as well get this over with.

They stepped into the cafeteria. The spacious room was half-filled with knots of chattering teachers, aides, office workers and other school personnel. At their appearance, Laney's worst fear was realized. Heads turned, and a hush fell over the crowd.

Then Ellen burst from the pack and hustled toward them. "Finally, they're here!"

Voices erupted in words of welcome as many surged toward Laney and Briana. Mouth hanging open, Laney was engulfed in a cheerful mob, and with Ellen's arm around her shoulders, ushered to the serving end of the cafeteria. They stopped before a table laden with goodies, but her eyes widened on the centerpiece—a sheet cake with words written on it in frosting.

We're with you, Laney and Briana!

A sob escaped Laney's throat, then another and another. Through tears, she barely recognized all the people who hugged her. She did miss one though—Noah. He stood on the fringe, smiling, but made no move to approach. Their gazes met, then his figure was blocked by a pair of male shoulders. She received a quick, tight hug, then looked up to see who had given it.

Pierce grinned down at her. "You're a popular lady. As you can see, no one's getting scared away from you by the boogie man."

Laney's mouth worked into a smile. Pierce meant well. If only this threat were really a figment of childish imagination. "How did you get out of driving bus this afternoon?" She didn't add, *What are you doing at a school staff party?* Ellen probably invited him. Her gaze found her friend standing nearby, and the dear, meddling woman had the cheek to wink at her.

Pierce shrugged. "It's my weekend to drive, so I had this Friday off. Couldn't think of anything better to do than lend my moral support to a special person."

A genuine smile bloomed on Laney's face. "I can hardly believe everyone's kindness."

"Come on." Pierce motioned her to follow him closer to the cake. "Let's get you the first piece." He turned. "Oops! I think your daughter beat you to it."

Ellen was ushering Briana past them toward a seat. The grinning little girl held a plate with a large chunk of chocolate-frosted marble cake perched on it. Her favorite! Laney shook her head. Ellen at work again.

Someone handed Laney the second piece, and then Pierce the third hunk. He took her elbow and escorted her at his usual leisurely pace toward the table where Briana and Ellen sat. He seated her, and then gave up his cake to the other woman at the table. The conspiratorial glance between the two wasn't lost on Laney. Then he withdrew to go back for a serving for himself.

She dropped her gaze and dug into her cake. Maybe she should consider giving Pierce a chance. He had good manners. She glanced toward him returning with another slice of cake. He was an attractive figure dressed in a striped sport shirt, crisp slacks, and new-looking leather shoes. Plus he was kind and obviously interested—whereas, Noah pointedly lacked that last qualification.

Where *was* the school principal? Laney looked around the room. Her gaze found Richard Hodge, who stood on the fringe of the festivities with his arms folded and the usual scowl on his face. Was he thinking about all the extra clean-up after this shindig? Or did he hate the love that was being shown to Laney and her daughter? Why would he feel that way about them? Hairs on her arms prickled. Hopefully, Noah could find something on him soon.

Laney continued to hunt for Noah, but didn't spot him anywhere. He'd left the party. She set her fork down, appetite gone. Why did her feelings have to run so strong for a man who saw her merely as a school district employee and now a client in his newly resurrected profession?

EIGHT

"That was a nice send-off the staff threw for you yesterday." From the aisle seat on the airplane, Noah smiled at Laney next to him. He could still see the stunned look on her face when she walked into the cafeteria.

Laney's color heightened. "I was totally humbled by the outpouring of love and encouragement, despite the trouble I brought to the school. Cottonwood Grove has great staff."

Noah nodded. "I think it's fair to say you're a well-liked team member. Hopefully, we can get this mess resolved soon so you can stay with us."

"Amen to that." Laney clasped her hands together. Then Briana claimed her attention.

They hadn't taken off yet, and the little girl had her nose pressed against the window, absorbing the sights on the runway. Laney had said this was Briana's first flight, and the child had been so proud, pulling her little princess wheeled suitcase to the gate and then onto the plane.

While Laney answered her daughter's questions, Noah shifted in his seat, seeking a comfortable position. But he was too wound up to find ease on a feather mattress, much less an airplane coach-class seat.

He'd observed their FBI tail follow them onto the aircraft—a stocky guy of medium height with dark hair and hard eyes set too close above a thin nose and thinner lips. If Noah didn't know better, he would've pegged the agent for a crook. Developing a similar look as the scum they chased was a hazard of the cop trade. The agent sat across the aisle and several seats behind them. Noah hadn't spotted anyone else following them, which is what he and the FBI had hoped would happen.

Frowning, he fidgeted with his seat belt as the engine revved up. He watched Laney out of the corner of his eye while she smiled and chattered with her excited daughter. They made an attractive picture.

Evidently, he wasn't the only one in Cottonwood Grove who agreed with that assessment. He could have done without that city bus driver hovering around Laney yesterday. The guy had it bad for the special ed teacher. Couldn't fault the man on his taste, though it would have been nice for Noah's sour grapes if he could have added the driver to his suspect list.

Noah had ducked out of the party and called the city office. The route log indicated Pierce was delivering elderly riders to the senior nutrition site at the time the backpack was left on the playground. Of course, Noah didn't blame the guy for knowing a good thing when he saw it. If attraction to Laney Thompson was a crime, they could lock Noah up and throw away the key.

Pretty soon they were taxiing down the runway, and then the plane left the ground. Briana squealed and laughed. Noah smiled and locked gazes with Laney.

"Not much scares her, does it?" he murmured to her. "Lots of adults are afraid to fly."

She gave a thin chuckle. "She's convinced God is watching over her."

"And you don't believe that?"

She sighed. "If anyone deserves a heavenly protector, Bree does. But then, I thought Gracie did, too."

"It's a puzzle, isn't it? Why bad things happen to the innocent?" A pang struck his chest, and he looked away.

He'd seen too much of that sort of injustice. What was he doing putting his soul on the firing line for possible tragedy again? Then he looked at Laney, her dark lashes shadowing sea-blue eyes, and her mirror image daughter so vibrant and happy. This pair trusted him. *Dear God, please, don't let me fail again!* He must be desperate. Here he was praying. His favorite motto used to be "God helps those who help themselves." Unfortunately, he'd learned too well what helplessness felt like.

"What?" he said. Laney had asked him something, but he'd missed her question.

"You must have had some training to become an expert private eye." She gazed at him expectantly.

Noah rolled his shoulders. "A little. After high school, I went to college and got a teaching certificate. Taught junior high math for a couple of years, but decided I wanted something with a little more excitement, so I went to the police academy."

"You're a cop?" Her eyes widened.

"I was. Spent two and a half years on the Minneapolis police force. Then a missing persons case came up that wouldn't let me go. I worked on it in all my spare time, and when that wasn't enough, I quit the force and took it on as a private case. After I solved that one, another case came along and then another and another, until—" He halted and cleared his throat. "Let's say I finally realized that there was something to be said for a career with less excitement."

Her lips flattened. "So you went back to school and got your principal's license."

"Good deduction." He chuckled.

"But the 'excitement,'" she bracketed the words with finger quotation marks, "followed you anyway. I'm sorry about that for your sake, but for ours, I've got enough faith to believe that God put you in the right place at the right time when Bree and I needed you."

The words struck him like a blow to the solar plexus. What about Renee? Where was the good plan then?

Laney breathed a deep sigh as they entered her parents' cool and elegant home from the hot and stuffy outside. They'd made it to Louisville without incident.

"There's my princesses!" her dad exclaimed, striding across the tiled foyer toward her and Briana. Noah trailed them with the luggage. Laney's mom had picked them up at the airport while her dad tied up a few loose ends at work, then raced home to be on hand when they arrived.

"Grandpa!" Briana scampered forward, and Laney smiled as her dad twirled her in the air. His broad, sun-bronzed face crinkled into fine lines of delight, and his blue eyes danced. He smacked a kiss onto her forehead, then set her down and turned toward Laney with his arms open wide. She stepped into them and rested her head on his thick shoulder.

Settling into her dad's warm embrace was coming home, even though the house wasn't like the ones she'd known in Minnesota. This home had a single floor, but plenty of square feet to include a spacious foyer, a sunken living room, a deluxe kitchen, a formal dining room, three bedrooms and two and a half baths, as well as a screened-in sunroom. Plus it sat on the edge of a golf course—

a dream home for a couple nearing retirement. Laney was glad for her father's big promotion that would let them end their working years in style, even though she missed them now that they lived so far away.

"Come on in and get settled," her mom said as Laney pulled away from her father. Her pretty, petite mother looked from Laney to Noah and back again. "Supper will be ready soon."

Noah sniffed the air. "Whatever it is smells delicious."

Laney's mother beamed. "Thank you. It's one of our little princess's favorites—roast chicken and stuffing."

"Oh, goodie!" Briana clapped her hands.

"Roland, why don't you show Mr. Ryder to his room." Mom nodded toward her husband. "Laney can take Briana and their things to their room while I set the table."

"Sounds like a plan." Dad flashed thumbs-up, then motioned toward their male guest.

"Call me Noah," Laney heard him tell her dad as they went up the hall. She took her daughter's hand and went in the other direction to a guest bedroom done in soft greens and mauves.

Fifteen minutes later, they shared the chicken dinner, and conversation remained light, but Laney intercepted sober looks between her parents. They must be on pins and needles to speak to Noah about his plans for the investigation. Briana's presence kept the adults tiptoeing around the pink elephant lounging in the middle of the table. Except for Noah. He seemed to be in high spirits as he teased and laughed with Briana.

Laney noticed her mother's assessing brown stare on Noah, weighing him for husband and daddy material like she did any male who came around her daughter. When her gaze switched to Laney, Laney's face heated, and she looked away, but not before she caught the barest lift of her mother's fine, dark brows. Great! As far as Mom's eagle eye was concerned, she might as well have a neon sign stuck to her forehead blinking *I'm into Noah.*

The evening wore on to Briana's bedtime. Laney tucked her daughter in and came out to find her parents with Noah in the sunken living room. She descended the two steps onto the plush carpet and took a seat near them on a divan. Her parents sat together on the couch, holding hands. Their tense gazes never left Noah, who nodded toward her. He had a manila envelope on his lap and was showing them pictures of Eddie Foreman, Richard Hodge and Glen Crocker.

Her father planted big hands on his knees. "Nope. We don't know any of these guys."

"I've redone a background check on this guy that we hired to be school custodian at the same time as we offered Laney a teaching contract." He showed Hodge's photo. "No new information came to light. His former employers call him a quiet man with a negative disposition but an excellent work ethic and good skills."

Loretta leaned forward. "Is it significant that this Hodge came on at the school at the same time as our daughter?"

"Sharp question." Noah smiled, and Loretta's pinched expression softened.

She must like Noah. Laney's insides warmed. Her mother's approval meant a lot to her.

"I noticed the coincidence, too," Noah continued. "But if he's our perp that raises the question of why he waited until the end of the school year to begin his terror campaign. I haven't answered that one, but I did look into where he was at the time of Grace's disappearance." Noah cast a significant look at his audience.

"And?" Laney's father rubbed his palms together.

"He was a teenage runaway with no known address. Basically, only he knows what he was doing from a period shortly before Grace's abduction until at least a year afterward, when his traceable work record begins."

Laney clasped her knees in her hands. "Where did he live before he ran away?"

"Near Hennepin Avenue in the heart of Minneapolis."

Roland frowned. "Not a good neighborhood."

Noah shook his head. "But that background might account for a dark outlook on life."

"Anything else?" Laney's dad prompted.

"I'm particularly interested in this one as a suspect." Noah held up the photo of Glen Crocker, then glanced over at Laney. "On Friday, my contact faxed me what little was in the record about an old, unclosed case."

Laney's parents exchanged questioning looks, and Noah filled them in about the electrician's unexplained disappearance from Cottonwood Grove. "Turns out that sixteen years ago Crocker was accused of assaulting the fifteen-year-old daughter of a city councilman in Red Wing, Minnesota."

Laney's mother stiffened. "Red Wing is only a couple hours' drive from Grand Valley."

Her father frowned. "Now, Loretta, that doesn't mean he was anywhere near our house the day Gracie went missing."

"No, it doesn't," Noah agreed. "But the incident puts Crocker within easy driving distance and exhibiting a taste for young girls."

Laney's stomach twisted, and her mother clamped a hand over her mouth.

Her father smacked his thigh. "Didn't this pervert get sent to prison?"

Noah shook his head. "He took a sudden trip to South America before the case could go to court, and stayed there until the statute of limitations ran out."

"So Crocker never felt any consequences?" Her father's meaty face blazed red.

"Unless you count seven years in Brazil as consequences."

Mom rubbed a hand down her cheek. "Won't they arrest this terrible man for Gracie?"

Noah shook his head. "There's not enough evidence. Besides, he's still missing."

Laney's father let out a husky snort while her mother wilted beside him.

"Maybe he went and got the backpack," Laney said, "and left it for me to find. Then he dressed up and delivered the doll, and now he's gone back to Brazil."

Noah sent her a sober look. "Hank's looking into that angle, but the taunts against you have been targeted and vindictive, which makes me wonder if Gracie's disappearance was a personal vendetta."

"You mean, not the random act of a stranger." Laney crossed her arms. "We've been over that territory already. Nobody had it in for our family."

Her mother bit her lip and studied the carpet, and her father's face went hard and still.

"Our daughter's right," he affirmed. "I've never had so much as a business rival."

Noah frowned, looking from one parent to the other. "Are you sure you never met Glen? Or maybe he had relatives in Grand Valley."

Laney's father shook his head. "There were no Crockers in Grand Valley. I'm convinced, as was the FBI eighteen years ago, that our daughter was the victim of a stranger abduction."

"Okay."

Laney bit her lip. Noah's word put him in agreement, but his tone telegraphed doubt. Heat washed through her. How dare he imply that her folks might not be telling the truth? He obviously didn't know them. The realization dashed cold water on her outrage, and she puffed out a breath. He'd acknowledge his mistake if he hung around her family for long. Wouldn't that be terrific if he got that chance after this mess was sorted out? A little thrill tingled up her spine.

"Noah," she said, "if any of us knew of a reason why someone would want revenge on our family, we'd tell you." There, that came out much better than snapping his head off like she might have done a few seconds ago.

He sent her a small smile. "I have no doubt you would."

Was the emphasis on *you* in that sentence? There she went again, being touchy about her family. This whole subject of Gracie's abduction made her skittish. The discussion was hard on everyone, judging by the strained looks her parents exchanged.

"Fair enough." Noah set the file aside. "Loretta, Roland, I'd like to hear in your own words exactly what happened the day Gracie disappeared. No detail is too insignificant." He pulled a pen and a small notebook from his shirt pocket.

Laney suffered through her folks' rendition of

events, not much different than her own, except from a parental point of view, rather than a child's. Not a hint of blame came from their lips toward her. The unsolicited—and undeserved—generosity of spirit ate at her. Now could they not see that she'd been at fault? Instead, all she heard was their heartfelt gratitude that she had not disappeared along with Gracie.

Laney's dark mood lasted through an ancient rerun of *Gilligan's Island,* which they all watched to unwind, followed by the news. In bed that night, she tried to lie still so as not to wake Briana, who slumbered peacefully next to her. *Gracie, we* have *to catch your killer.* Maybe if justice was finally served, she could forgive herself and move on with life, minus the guilt that dragged on her soul like a ball and chain.

NINE

The next morning, Noah got ready to leave on a flight back to Minnesota and a fact-finding mission to the Thompson's old stomping grounds where the abduction took place. Last night's conversation bothered him. Laney couldn't, or wouldn't, see it, but something had happened in Grand Valley that neither of her parents wanted to talk about. But that didn't mean the veiled history was connected to Grace's disappearance. Surely, Laney's parents would speak up if there was even a remote chance that it might be.

They seemed a close-knit couple and adored their daughter and granddaughter. When she greeted them at the airport, petite Loretta Thompson had sized him up with a fierce look that told him he'd better be the real deal as an investigator and a stand-up kind of guy in the way he treated her loved ones. *Yes, ma'am!* Noah grinned as he tucked his shaving kit into his carry-on. He wasn't about to do anything to antagonize a ferocious mama bear.

Roland was actually built like a bear, thick and solid, with a booming laugh and a friendly manner. But he was an astute businessman and as determined as his wife to protect his own. While Laney put Briana to bed last night and Loretta did a few things in the kitchen, they'd retired to the living room for a serious discussion.

"I've had you thoroughly vetted," the man had told him. "My sources tell me you used to be the best, but nobody's offered me a clear explanation for why you quit."

Noah shrugged. "I guess there's only so much tragedy a person can witness until it comes time to change the scenery."

Roland frowned and nodded. "Fair enough." His gaze turned assessing. "I suppose the better question would be what drew you out of retirement."

"I guess you could call it the case that landed in my backyard." Noah grimaced. "When your daughter asked for my help, I could hardly turn her down."

The other man grinned. "I never could turn down those big blue eyes of hers, either."

If Noah could have stopped the heat from rising in his face he would have.

Laney's father laughed and offered his big bear paw. "Just so you know, I'd pay double your price to get the best for my daughter."

Noah had gladly shaken Roland's hand.

Now he zipped his suitcase with a frown. The man didn't seem like the kind to make lethal enemies, but then, appearances could be deceiving. Of course, anyone could run afoul of a psycho and set him off for no rational reason. Noah would keep an open mind when he started asking questions of the natives in the Thompson's old hometown.

He pulled his case into the kitchen where the family waited for him, all but Briana, who was still sleeping at the 7:00 a.m. hour. Roland sipped coffee at the oval table with the newspaper spread before him. Loretta stood stirring scrambled eggs. They both looked up and greeted him with smiles. Laney's dad motioned to a spot next to him.

"You're all ready?" Laney whisked past him carrying plates and forks toward the table. Her blue gaze held a hint of sadness.

Because he was leaving? Noah's heart jumped but he commanded it to settle back into place. She had plenty of other reasons to be sad, as well as for the weariness betrayed by the droop of her shoulders.

He touched her arm as he took his seat. "Get some rest while you're in a safe haven."

She laughed, and tension retreated from her face. "Is it that obvious? I don't think I've enjoyed a decent sleep since I found that pack."

Roland grabbed his daughter's hand. "You just settle in here, honey, and let us look after you.

Noah can do the legwork. Maybe he'll come up with something those duded up FBI agents missed."

Noah's chest expanded under warm scrutiny from three pairs of eyes. *God, make me worthy of this trust.* Maybe if he'd leaned more on the Lord, instead of his own abilities, that other case might have turned out better.

The foursome settled at the table over an eggs and toast breakfast. Roland bowed his head and extended his hands. His wife and daughter each took one, while Noah accepted the delicate hands of the women and lowered his head. Noah might have been able to concentrate better on the prayer if an electric charge didn't seem to run between his and Laney's joined fingers, but he appreciated this family's steady faith after what they'd been through. Sometimes families fell apart during tragedy; other times they got stronger. Noah wasn't sure yet what his deep loss had done to the faith his parents had taught him. He was still on rocky ground, undecided where he was at with God…or God with him.

Roland concluded the prayer, and everyone released hands. Laney's smooth palm slid away from his, and Noah felt the absence. He kept his eyes averted from hers and concentrated on his plate. The steaming eggs sent delicious smells to his nostrils. The doorbell rang, and he halted with a forkful of eggs halfway to his open mouth. He exchanged looks with Roland. Who would come calling so early on a Sunday morning?

Laney's father headed for the door. Murmured voices, Roland's and an unknown female's, carried to Noah's ears. A few seconds later, Roland appeared with a stocky woman beside him. Noah recognized the law enforcement prowl in her walk and the sweep of her eyes across the room, taking in every detail. She was likely on Laney and Briana's Louisville watch detail. But why had she blown cover to waltz through the front door?

The woman flashed an FBI badge, confirming Noah's assumption. "I'm here to inform you that an arrest has been made in your case."

A soft cry came from Loretta, while Laney gripped the edge of the table. "Who?" she burst out.

"Edward Foreman."

Noah's heart skipped a beat, and then he frowned. "On what grounds?" The evidence had to be substantial in order to make an actual arrest.

"I'm not at liberty to tell you that, sir. Would you be Noah Franklin Ryder?"

"Guilty." He lifted a palm.

An almost-smile flickered at the corners of the agent's mouth. "I have a message for you from Supervisory Special Agent Burns."

Noah snorted. "I can about guess what that is."

The agent's lips curved up another millimeter. "He says to go back to the day job. The professionals have done their work."

"And you can tell him—" Noah stopped himself from questioning the arrest. "Never mind."

He wasn't about to rain on the parade of relieved grins from Roland, Loretta and Laney. But until he knew what evidence they were charging Eddie on, he wouldn't be convinced they had the right man. Granted, he had his own doubts about the playground skulker, but a solid case should take longer than this to build.

Roland escorted the agent out while Laney and her mother grabbed each other and wept. Noah studied his cooling eggs.

Laney's father returned to the table, rubbing his hands together and beaming. "Looks like we won't need to disrupt your life any further, Noah. We appreciate your willingness to help us out and the care you've taken of Laney and the little Breebee." He slapped Noah on the back.

Noah rose and shook the man's hand, forcing a smile onto his face. "I hope this is the closure your family needs."

Laney came around the table and touched his arm. Her cheeks glistened with happy tears, but her gaze telegraphed concern. "You look more troubled than happy."

He sighed. "I have a lot of questions—"

"Oh, me, too!" Laney twirled in a little dance across the tile floor, and Noah's pulse leaped at her unconscious grace. "Simply to know Gracie's killer is finally in custody and Briana is safe means everything! I can get my hundred and one questions answered later."

"At least let me make a phone call to Hank and see if he has an inkling what hard evidence brought about the arrest."

"Please do." Loretta gripped the back of her chair. "We'd all like to know."

Noah took out his cell phone and went into the living room. A few minutes later, he returned to the kitchen. The family had gone back to their seats, but it looked as if the excitement had stolen their appetites. Their plates remained full. Hopeful faces turned toward him.

He awarded them a nod and a smile. "Hank has his own resources for finding out what's going on with the feds, and the collar looks good to him. Traces of Eddie's blood were found on the backpack, and a personal history check shows he had a route delivering office supplies that covered southeastern Minnesota at the time of Grace's abduction."

Laney slumped and lowered her forehead to the table, weeping again. "Thank you, Lord Jesus," she breathed.

"Hallelujah!" Loretta clapped her hands.

Roland grinned bigger than the Cheshire cat. "I guess you've got no reason to travel to Grand Valley now. You can head straight for home once you reach Minneapolis." He looked at his watch. "We'd better get a move on if you're going to catch your flight."

"Oh, dear." Loretta stood, and Laney with her. "I'm sorry you didn't get breakfast."

"No problem." Noah waved a hand. "I'll grab something at the airport."

Laney glided toward him and stopped close enough for her fresh scent to wrap around his senses. "Thank you."

The depth of gratitude in her gaze for the nothing he had done humbled Noah's soul. "I'm very happy for you. Will I see you in the fall?"

She laughed. "Only if you put in that recommendation for me to the school board."

"Consider it a done deal." He grinned down at her, then followed Roland toward the door. His smile faded. Should he get their hopes up by telling them the bonus information Hank shared with him? Maybe it would be best if he told Laney's father only and let him make the call of what to say to his wife and daughter.

They got on the road, and Roland drove intently and quickly. Laney's father must be itching to get back to his family for a personal time of rejoicing. Running a guest to the airport was a necessary inconvenience. Maybe soon they'd have something more to celebrate.

"I didn't want to say anything too soon," Noah began, "but Hank had more to tell."

Roland glanced at Noah, and the car's speed slackened. "Good news? Bad news?"

"The dirt on the backpack was consistent with

the soil found in the Grand Valley area. The FBI is cautiously optimistic that when this guy confesses, he'll be able to point them to a grave site near where you used to live."

Roland pumped a fist. "Finally we can put Gracie properly to rest!"

Noah looked out the side window at glistening hotels and office complexes whisking past. He'd wanted to say "if" the guy confesses. If only Noah could feel as confident as everyone else that the case was closed. Edward Foreman was a stranger to the Thompsons, as was true in many pedophile abduction situations. He would have no personal ties to the family that would create rage in his mind. Why then had the taunts toward Laney been so calculated and vicious?

After church followed by a meal out, Laney walked into the house, yawning. Exhaustion had closed in—partly from poor sleep for many days, and partly as a backlash from euphoria.

Her mother laughed. Laney hadn't seen her mom so bright and cheerful in years. The woman practically glowed. "You lie down and take a nap, dear. Your dad and I will keep both sets of eyes on the little Bree-bee."

Her father seconded the motion. He'd joined them at church barely in time for service to start. He swung Briana's hand in his. "How about we go to the zoo and let your mommy sleep?"

She hopped up and down. "Monkeys. I want to see the monkeys."

"The ape exhibit can be our first stop." He tapped the end of his granddaughter's nose.

"You mind Grandma and Grandpa now," Laney admonished, shaking her head. Children were so resilient. Her daughter had casually received the information that the bad man had been caught, but she'd pouted about Noah leaving. Now she was excited.

Eyelids drooping, Laney wandered into the bedroom and curled up under a light blanket in the air-conditioned coolness. Her groggy thoughts drifted to Noah. He'd be in the air now, traveling away from her. If only he'd shown half a moment's interest in staying for a visit. Her folks would have welcomed him, and in a relaxed social setting, maybe she would have stood a chance of catching his interest as more than a colleague or a client.

Ever on the lookout for husband material for her daughter, Mom had read too much into Noah's promise of a recommendation to the school board. "That man wants to keep you around," she had said with a knowing nod right before church service got under way. "Of course, he does," Laney'd whispered back. "Special education teachers aren't easy to come by." Mom slanted her an amused look. "There are none so blind as those who will not see." Then the worship team moved into the opening song, and the subject was dropped.

Laney prayed that by some miracle her mother was right about Noah, and that Noah was wrong in his reservations about Edward Foreman's guilt. She could tell he still wasn't satisfied about that when he left. Foreman *had* to be guilty. A stranger abduction made perfect sense. Couldn't Noah see that? This nightmare needed to be over. *Please, God!*

Her consciousness faded with her prayer. The next thing she knew, she opened her eyes, and the bedside clock said three thirty-two. She'd slept for two glorious, refreshing hours. She sat up and stretched her arms. Stone silence in the house indicated that her parents and Briana lingered at the zoo. Wouldn't it be nice if she had a yummy supper prepared when they got home?

Energized, Laney hopped out of bed. She placed a quick call to her dad's cell phone. He answered on the third ring and assured her Briana was having the time of her life and never out of their sight. Laney bit her lip. The hard lesson learned with Gracie would never fade, even though her killer was in custody.

"Tell Mom not to worry about supper. I'm on my way to the store for taco fixings."

Dad chuckled. "Bree's going to think it's her birthday. The zoo and now tacos."

Laney gave an answering laugh. "I've got a good guess where she gets her taste buds. Sometimes I think you should have been born south of the border."

They ended the call. Laney ran a comb through her hair and brushed her teeth, and then grabbed her purse and the keys to her mom's car from the hook in the laundry room. An hour later, she pulled back into the driveway of her parents' home with two sacks of groceries sitting next to her in the passenger seat.

She mashed the button on the automatic garage door opener, but got no response. She tried again, and the door still didn't budge. Oh, bother! The batteries were probably dead. Good thing the ring for the car keys also held a house key. She shut the vehicle off and went around to the passenger side to collect her groceries.

As she leaned in to grab them, a soft shuffling sound carried to her from behind. She stiffened and began to turn. A hard object crashed into the back of her head, and bright sunshine faded to twilight as she folded to the pavement. A torn tennis shoe swam into view. Then darkness owned her.

TEN

The hum of tires against the pavement and mellow classic rock turned low on the radio kept Noah company on the road between Minneapolis and Cottonwood Grove. He should have chosen a blues station to reflect his mood. As much as he'd resisted taking another missing person's case, he'd begun to taste the thrill of the hunt. A shameful, selfish little gremlin on the inside felt cheated of the catch.

Worse, Laney and Briana were out of this life—at least for the summer. There was no guarantee they would return to Cottonwood Grove in the fall. With Laney's parents living in Louisville, it would be easy for her to decide to take a job in that area.

Driving through one of the myriad small towns along Highway 55, his cell phone rang. He turned off into a convenience store parking lot and answered.

"This is Roland Thompson," said the voice at the other end.

The gravity in the man's tone sat Noah to attention. "What's up?"

"Laney's been attacked."

Bile scorched the back of Noah's throat. He swallowed. "Is she all right?"

"We're at the hospital with her now. She's got a concussion, and they're admitting her overnight for observation—over her protests, I might add." Roland heaved a harsh breath. "Her memory is pretty fuzzy, but she thinks somebody came up behind her in our driveway and clubbed her over the head. We believe—" The man's voice broke. "We believe that's all that happened, but they're checking her out more thoroughly."

White heat flashed through Noah. "I'm turning around. I'll catch the first flight." He shot out of the parking lot. Somebody was going to answer for this.

"Thank you." The words came out laden with emotion. "We don't have the right guy behind bars yet, do we." The sentence was a statement, not a question.

"It would appear not." Noah pressed the gas pedal until his speed hovered on the edge of demanding a cop's attention. "Have you notified the FBI?"

"There's an agent here breathing fire down our necks to talk to her, but the doc hasn't let him in yet."

"I'll call Sheriff Lindoll in Cottonwood Grove

and see if he can get a feel for what's happening in the Minneapolis office as a result of this development."

"Thanks again, Noah. A boulder just rolled off my chest, knowing you're back on the case. Laney will be happy to see you, too." The tone held a sly note.

What was Laney's father trying to tell him?

"My wife's pretty sharp about these things, and she insists you care for my daughter," Roland added. "Is she right?" The point-blank question said the man would stand for no evasion.

So that was it. Noah might as well own up. "Yes, sir, I do. But I don't plan to let personal feelings affect how I handle this matter."

"See that you don't. Let it ride…for now."

Hope skimmed Noah's consciousness. Was the man hinting his daughter might return the interest? Laney had always been reserved and professional around him. And then there was Pierce vying for her affection, and she wasn't exactly pushing him away.

"Expect me this evening," he told Roland, and they ended the call.

Noah punched in the auto dial for Hank. Good thing he'd programmed that number in before he left home.

"We've got trouble," Hank greeted him.

"You know already?"

"What are you talking about? You can't possibly know what I know."

Noah took a deep breath. "Let's start this conversation over. Laney was struck from behind outside her parents' home, and she's in the hospital. Is that the trouble you mean?"

Hank let out a low whistle. "No, it sure isn't. She all right?"

"Concussion. They're checking her out at the hospital now."

"Someone popping Laney makes my information even more vital."

Noah's hands strangled the steering wheel. "What bomb are you sitting on, Lindoll?"

"Your school custodian has disappeared. Miss Aggie phoned me about a couple hours ago when he didn't answer an emergency call about what could be a burst pipe in the school building. It's a regular flood, pouring out the doors onto the sidewalks. That's how some neighbors noticed it on a Sunday and all."

Noah groaned. Great! A crisis at the school, too. "Maybe Richard's out of town for the weekend."

"That's what I thought at first, but I got curious, so I drove to that farm place he rents outside of town." Hank's desk chair creaked in the background. "The door to the house was standing wide open. Everything's gone—personal effects, furniture, the little horse trailer he used when he moved his stuff in, the whole nine yards. I hate to tell you, but your custodian has moved on without notice."

Noah scratched behind his ear with his thumb as

he held the phone. "Maybe the landlord knows where he went."

"Ahead of you there." The sheriff gave a dry chuckle. "He had no idea the guy was moving out and stiffing him for a month's rent, much less where his tenant was headed."

Noah's gut clenched. "Maybe Louisville, Kentucky."

"I've got an APB out on his vehicle, as well as a request for the Minneapolis PD to check the airport lots."

Noah nodded, though he realized the other man couldn't see him. "Have you tapped your source in the federal office to see what they're thinking about Edward Foreman now that Laney's been attacked while he's in custody? The guy's blood on the backpack begs an explanation."

Hank's chair creaked. "I'd give a lot to know what Foreman says about how that blood got there, if he's innocent the way they all say."

"Could there be conspirators?" Noah burst out with the first thing that came to his head. "But then," he added, as arguments against the theory rushed him, "pedophiles don't normally work together. If we're actually dealing with that sort of monster. I've been toying with other ideas—like a vendetta against the Thompson family. But why has there been an eighteen-year span of time between attacks?"

Hank grunted. "I'm leaning toward the lone pedophile angle. Maybe the perp socked Laney over the head to get her out of the way, thinking her daughter was in the car."

Noah's brows lifted. "That's a good theory. I may know more when I talk to Laney."

"And I'll get what I can out of the feds."

"I'm on my way back to Louisville. If that's where our perp is, that's where I need to be, flooded school or not. I'll have to call Miss Aggie for an update on that end."

"You do that." Hank chuckled. "Chances are she gave that flood water one of her looks, and it high-tailed straight back into the pipe it came from."

Noah spurted a laugh. "That wouldn't surprise me."

He hung up with Hank and got on the phone to the school office. If he guessed correctly, that's where he'd find his ever-capable assistant. She answered on the second ring.

"Are you up to your neck in alligators?" Noah asked her.

"Hah!" she barked. "That's about the only thing we don't have around here, what with the plumber, the insurance adjuster and the clean-up crew."

"How bad is the damage?" He passed a sign that said he was nearing Minneapolis. He'd be back at the airport in about forty-five minutes, barring traffic issues.

"The adjuster hasn't said yet. At minimum we'll need a new gym floor, as well as some sheet rocking where water soaked up the sides of the walls."

Noah shook his head. "For the water to have saturated that much, the pipe must have burst shortly after we locked up the building on Friday."

"Who said a pipe burst?" Her words contained an edge.

"Well," Noah paused, "Hank mentioned that as a speculation."

Miss Aggie sniffed. "A lot he knows. I got a plumber in here right away. He says somebody turned on the main and left it running."

Words dried up in Noah's throat. Someone had sabotaged the school building, *and* someone had struck Laney *and* someone had abducted and killed a defenseless child eighteen years ago. The same person? Richard Hodge? Noah's brow furrowed.

The custodian had been rifling through the backpack when Noah came outside to secure the scene. Had the man been trying to convey the appearance of natural curiosity as a cover for a deeper motive—to give a non-suspicious reason for why his prints or DNA might be on the pack? Then how did Edward Foreman's blood end up on Grace's school bag? This case grew more confusing by the minute.

Laney lay in a hospital bed with the head end elevated, and stared without seeing at a television program. She gnawed at her lower lip. Why couldn't she be home with her parents and her daughter, instead of stuck in an institution for a night? Except for a nagging headache, masked by a painkiller, she was fine. Physically, anyway.

Her dad had been torn, wanting to bunk here in her room and play guard dog and needing to watch over Briana, too. Her mom had offered to stay in the hospital while dad went with Briana, but Laney shooed them all away. Who could get to her with an FBI muscleman stationed outside her door? Now, Laney regretted her choice as she stared at four walls in a lonely room.

Who was doing these awful things? Edward Foreman was off the hook—at least, for today's assault. Was the real perp after her, or was he trying to get through her to Briana? If the creep was after her daughter, why warn her with these taunts? Why not go straight to the snatch? Something didn't add up. Maybe Noah was right that more was going on here than a simple case of stranger abduction. But if the attacks were personal, why? Laney's stomach knotted.

Her bedside telephone rang, and Laney jerked upright, bringing a pulse of pain from her head. She expelled a breath. Probably mom calling to say good-night. She picked up the receiver. "Hello."

Harsh, heavy breathing responded. Laney's skin crawled.

"See how the players pay when the innocents suffer?" a male voice grated in her ear.

Laney's mouth went dry as sun-baked tarmac. A click announced that the connection had closed.

"Wait!" She found her voice, but empty air mocked her.

A sharp rap sounded on the hospital room door, and it began to ease open. Had this creep gotten past the agent outside? Laney let out a shriek. The receiver fell from nerveless fingers and clattered to the linoleum. Male shouts of alarm responded and two men burst into the room—one the burly agent, the other familiar and welcome.

"Oh, Noah!" Laney cried. "I just had the most horrible phone call." She held out her arms. He sat on the edge of her bed and held her while tears wet his shirt. "I can't—do this—anymore. It has—to stop!"

"Shh…shh. We'll make it stop. Don't worry. We'll get the guy."

Noah's tenderly spoken assurances soothed Laney's heart, and his arms cocooned her soul. If only this moment could last forever. But of course it couldn't. In fact, she was making a complete fool of herself. With a sigh, Laney pulled away. Eyes down, she picked at her sheet with thumb and forefinger.

Noah's hand cupped her chin. "Tell us what happened."

Her gaze found the agent standing beyond Noah, and heat seared her cheeks. Bad enough that she'd lost control with Noah, but a witness compounded the embarrassment with interest.

"Someone called you on the telephone, ma'am?" the agent prompted.

She nodded and returned her attention to Noah, who stood up and backed away a step. She'd probably made him terribly uncomfortable with her hysterical display.

"It was a man," she said. "I didn't recognize the voice, but he whispered in this harsh tone, so maybe he was trying to disguise his voice."

Noah bent toward her. "What did he say?"

"Something about innocents paying… No, that's not right. I don't—" She closed her eyes and fished for the exact memory among her jumbled thoughts. That blow to the head must have done more damage than she realized. "He said, 'See how the players pay when the innocents suffer?'" She opened her eyes.

The agent nodded, gaze distant. He pulled out a cell phone and strode from the room.

"Good job." Noah smiled at her. "We'll let the federal guys try to figure out where that call came from, but I doubt they'll have any luck."

"What do you think that man meant by players paying? Like gambling?"

"I don't know, Laney. Maybe your parents will have an idea."

She scowled up at him. There he went again with the insinuations. "Why should they have a clue? Neither of them has a gambling problem."

Noah's gaze remained tender against hers. "Then there must be another meaning."

Laney's hands fisted. "Every time I turn around some new taunt blindsides me."

"You said a mouthful there." He frowned. "The focus seems to be on you, and the attacks are escalating to physical now. I agree. This has to end pronto."

Laney sat forward. "Do you think this creep isn't after Briana after all?" The notion brought up a whole new train of thought of a way to help protect her daughter and work toward catching this guy at the same time.

"I can't say that yet." Noah scratched under his ear. "Extreme precautions need to be taken with her, as well."

Laney nodded. "My dad has hired private security guards on top of whatever the FBI has on us. He told me he's upgrading his security system at home tomorrow, too."

"Good for him. You should be pretty safe holed up there until this is over."

She lifted her chin. "I'm not 'holing up,' as you put it. If this guy wants me, then I'm going to make him come after me…away from my daughter."

Noah's brow knotted. "What are you talking about?"

"Humor me for a minute while I explain my logic." She held up a palm at his skeptical expression. "The backpack was left for me to find. Only I would know its significance. Then the doll was sent to me. And you know what?" She snapped her fingers. "Bree has light brown hair. The doll was blonde like Grace. This guy really *is* after me. It's like he's trying to finish what he started. Maybe he intended to take us both the day he got Gracie."

Her breath caught. Could it be that her irresponsible behavior had spared her life after all? That her parents were right to be thankful she wasn't with Grace that day? She shook her head. What if she'd been able to save them both if she hadn't run off and left her sister alone to deal with a monster?

"Earth to Laney."

Noah's voice jerked her attention back to the present. "Sorry. I was following a rabbit trail. The bottom line is this." She folded her hands together on her lap. "If this guy wants me, I'm going to make him come after me. We're going to end this nightmare once and for all…back in Grand Valley, where the horror started."

If she'd exploded a bomb in his face, Noah couldn't have looked any more shell-shocked.

ELEVEN

Briana snuggled next to Noah as he read her a storybook in her grandparents' living room that evening. How could anyone even think about hurting someone so cute and precious and innocent? He'd always been outraged that monsters existed who targeted children, but this little girl was special—as special as her mom.

Noah closed the book, and the child looked up at him and smiled. "I'm glad you came back, Mr. Ryder. Can you stay now?"

He ruffled her soft hair. "I'm afraid I have to return to Minnesota tomorrow. Your mother is coming with me. Are you okay with that?"

Laney's parents weren't. They'd rushed to the hospital to see their daughter when they heard about the phone call, and a long and heated discussion had ensued at Laney's bedside while the federal agent entertained Briana in the hallway by showing her his badge. At least that's what Noah had caught him doing when he checked on them.

A margin of calm had descended between Laney and her parents when Noah updated them that law enforcement was hot on the trail of Richard Hodge. In the end, Noah had come back to the Thompson's home with an agitated Roland while Loretta insisted on staying the night with Laney at the hospital.

Briana looked untroubled by the prospect of her mother leaving. She pursed her lips, then nodded. "If you're with Mama, then it's okay. The bad man won't get her then."

Noah's rib cage squeezed in on itself. He'd better be up to the challenge…this time. Or die trying. There was no way he could look into this child's face, or his own in the mirror, if he let anything happen to Laney.

He fully sympathized with her parents' reservations about the plan. His heart had hit the floor when Laney said she was going with him. How did he let her talk him into taking her along anyway? Roland was right about those big blue eyes. Plus, she'd produced a surprising stubborn streak wider than the Mississippi Delta. But the reasons went beyond that. Her proposal made sense, as much as he hated for her to continue to act as bait. Whoever was doing this had it in for her, and he wasn't going to stop until he was caught.

A half hour later, Briana was tucked into bed, and Noah told Roland he was heading there himself. He was exhausted.

The other man sent him a long look. "My granddaughter adores you. I'm a little jealous. I've never seen her like that with another man." He lifted a brow. "Tread carefully. You seem to be working your way into the hearts of some important ladies in my life, and I don't want to see them hurt."

Noah swallowed against a dry throat. "Believe me, I don't, either."

In bed, he tossed and turned, seeking sleep that lurked beyond his reach. Was there a chance for him and Laney when this was over? She'd felt so right in his arms when he held her at the hospital. If he could move beyond the past, maybe he could take a chance on a future with an attractive special ed teacher and her charming little girl. And he wanted more kids, too, if he were honest with himself. But until this murderous scum was caught, none of them would have the opportunity to find out what might be. Until then, he needed to keep his mind off romance. Hadn't he learned his lesson about that the hard way?

He fell into a doze, and dreams of Renee teased him. Her tall, lithe figure flitted past his mind's eye. Her laughter caressed his ears. Then she stood before him clear and strong and smiling. "Goodbye, my darling." Her brown gaze sifted him. She turned and walked away, and he let her.

He opened his eyes the next morning to the gray haze of dawn filtering around the window shades. Something was different. His senses perked up.

No, not in his surroundings. Inside himself. Something bound up tight in his core had begun to unfurl. The feeling was scary and exhilarating at the same time. Could he really move on from Renee? If he'd never met Laney and her sweet little Briana, he probably wouldn't even be considering it.

But that was the point. Right now, he needed to quit thinking about it. Unfortunately for his peace of mind, the task of reining in his attraction to Laney was about as simple as herding cats. How could he be with her constantly in Grand Valley and not give away how he felt?

Noah groaned and got out of bed and headed for the shower. *Lord, if you're there for me at all, I could use a truckload of help staying sharp and focused on what matters—catching the creep that threatens these precious people's lives.*

Soon Loretta brought her daughter home to pack her luggage. Laney spent long minutes bidding Briana farewell, and the child had a big hug for Noah. Roland watched the leave-taking with his arms crossed and lowered brows, while Loretta flitted around fussing about whether Laney remembered to take this or that.

Finally they piled into the car. Loretta drove, and Laney rode shotgun. In the backseat Noah kept an eye out for anyone who might be following them. All he spotted was the unmarked federal sedan he'd picked out almost as soon as they left the driveway. Conversation was sporadic, and Laney's mother fidgeted with her hair and her clothes and the air conditioning and the radio.

Casual topics of conversation were in short supply, but the mundane seemed like an insult to the situation. If only he'd get word from Hank that they'd cornered Richard Hodge. But Noah's phone remained stubbornly silent.

Laney had been as baffled as her parents why the custodian had it in for the school, much less why he might have been Grace's kidnapper all those years ago. Noah's inquiries into Hodge's background didn't flag the tendencies of a pedophile, so lack of motive made a flimsy case for the kidnapping, though opportunity and attitude made him suspect number one in the flooding. They'd have to wait until the man was caught to find out more.

Seated at the gate waiting for their flight to be called, Noah's phone rang, and his pulse jumped. It was Hank. "What've you got for me?"

Next to him, Laney stopped leafing through a magazine and stared at him.

"No sign of Hodge's vehicle at either airport in Minneapolis," the sheriff said. "I put out the word to the Sioux Falls PD, too. Some folks fly out of there."

Noah sighed. "I guess that's all you can do until someone spots him."

"That's not the end of the frustrating news,"

Hank growled. "They've released Edward Foreman. He remains a suspect, but the prosecutor refuses to take the case to court after what happened with Laney yesterday."

"I expected that much." Noah sniffed. "Did you find out what excuse Foreman gave for his blood on that backpack?"

"I played the 'need to know because this guy lives in our area' card and got a transcript of the interview with him from the feds." Papers rattled in the background. "Seems the guy finally admitted he *was* at the playground watching his daughter the day the pack was left. He pinched some skin off his finger when he gripped the chain link. Before he left that day, he spotted the pack sitting *outside* the fence. Good citizen that he is, he didn't want someone coming along and making off with it before the student could claim their property. So he picked it up, cut finger and all, walked over to the entrance opening and set it *inside* the fence, and then skedaddled."

Noah groaned and scrubbed a hand over his face. "If this guy's telling the truth, where the pack was found wasn't where it was left, and any forensic evidence collected from the grounds wasn't even from the right spot."

Hank clucked his tongue. "You win the award for tip-top deduction."

Noah informed the sheriff about Laney's twisted phone call last night and of his plans to visit Grand

Valley with her in tow. Hank told him to be careful, and they ended the call.

"I take it the news isn't the best," Laney prompted.

Noah grimaced and filled her in on what Hank said.

Without a word, she looked toward the gate desk. Noah followed her gaze. Increased activity warned that they'd be calling the flight soon.

"You know something?" she finally said. "I believe this Edward character is telling the truth. His story is goofy yet detailed enough to be exactly what happened."

"I hate to admit it." Noah frowned. "But you could be right." And there went a very promising suspect.

Now if only law enforcement could lay their hands on Richard Hodge and Glen Crocker. One of them could be the perp they were looking for, and then the ordeal would be over… And that could be the beginning of possibilities for him with Laney. He glanced at the delicate-framed, strong-spirited woman next to him. Her gaze was veiled behind long lashes as she studied her shoes.

Suddenly she jerked to attention. "I remember something about the attack."

Noah stiffened. "What is it?"

"The man's tennis shoes. The seam by the big toe of the left foot was splitting out."

"Exactly the problem with the fake postman's

shoe that Mattie described." Noah's breath caught. "The footwear must be more significant than a random piece of this perp's disguise."

Laney fixed a wide gaze on him. "We're looking for someone with a foot deformity. And I just thought of something else." She poked a finger at him. "Richard Hodge wore steel-toed shoes. I know. I tripped over them in the crowded office the day I found that backpack."

"And steel-toed shoes could hide a foot problem."

"Exactly." She smacked her palms together.

Tingles ran up Noah's spine. This was a hot lead. "I didn't know to ask former employers if they were aware that the man had any foot problems. I'll rectify the oversight when we get to the hotel in Grand Valley. Right now," he nodded toward the gate desk where the attendant had picked up the microphone, "I think our flight is about to be called."

When they finally reached Minneapolis and got on the road south toward Grand Valley, silence blanketed the vehicle. Laney studied Noah out of the corner of her eye. His gaze was intent on the ribbon of highway. Both hands gripped the steering wheel as if it might attempt to spring away from him at any moment. A muscle in his jaw jumped from time to time.

"Did we have an FBI watcher on the plane?" she asked. "I can't tell like you do."

He glanced at her, sober-faced. "An agent followed us to the gate, but stayed behind. One was noticeably absent when we debarked, but I suspect they're ahead of us at our destination. They're going to want to see if our perp makes a run at you again."

"I don't imagine Agent Burns is any too happy that you're in the picture."

Noah cracked a smile. "That's Supervisory Special Agent Burns to you." His tone mimicked the agent.

Laney laughed. "You already know how I met the guy and why I don't like him. You obviously have a history with him, too. Care to share?"

Noah's nostrils flared and the smile faded.

Laney looked down. She'd trodden on forbidden territory. "Sorry. That was nosy."

He shook his head. "No, it was a fair question from someone in your position. You should be aware of any history that might affect my performance on this case."

Laney's fingers curled around the seat edge. That's right, she was only a client to him. "No need to explain. Agent Burns is the sort of person who would rub anyone raw." And she needed to quit expecting Noah to open up to her. She was constantly setting herself up for disappointment that way.

"He got my fiancée killed."

Noah's quietly spoken words reverberated in Laney's ears. "He what?" She stared at him.

"I think he figures it the other way around. But then, I blame myself, too." He heaved a sigh.

Laney groaned. This must be the case where he'd told her "the wheels came off" and "someone died." Was that person his fiancée? How horrible! No wonder he'd no longer had the stomach for the P.I. business. What a miracle he'd taken her case.

"Do you remember hearing about the Halliday kidnapping around six years ago?" he asked.

"Who doesn't? A wealthy media mogul's seven-year-old daughter was taken right out of their heavily guarded Minneapolis lake home. National news went on and on about the incident." Laney gasped. "I remember your name being mentioned once or twice toward the end of the sad ordeal, but nothing about Burns."

Noah snorted. "The FBI likes to keep the names of field agents out of public awareness. They issue statements through staff hired for that purpose. But Burns was the lead investigator."

"Didn't they figure the nanny was in on the conspiracy to get the ransom?"

"A couple of problems with that information. First," Noah lifted a finger from the steering wheel, "the ransom demand was a farce to cover the real crime, and second," he lifted another finger, "the nanny was innocent."

Tumblers clicked into place in Laney's mind. "The nanny was your fiancée." She remembered tabloid photos staring at her from grocery checkout aisles, featuring a lovely fair-haired child and the dark-haired, exotic-featured woman suspected of kidnapping her.

Noah nodded. "Her name was Renee Jackson, and we weren't engaged when the case started. The FBI was hounding her, especially after the ransom was delivered, they didn't catch the perp, and the child wasn't returned."

"That state of affairs can't have sat well with Burns." A man as prickly about his reputation as the federal agent would have been rabid to make an arrest.

"That's an understatement." Noah rolled his eyes. "And he targeted Renee as his chief suspect. She came to me desperate to clear her name. Those big brown eyes of hers bored into my soul, and I was hooked. I took her on pro bono. A nanny doesn't have the money her rich employers do. Of course, Burns thought greed gave her motive."

Laney angled her body toward Noah. "So you believed her innocent right off the bat?"

"Let's just say, from what I'd heard through the grapevine about the case, I thought there were angles that needed to be checked. After Renee got me on board, the more I looked into things, the more I was convinced she'd been set up and by whom. My big mistake was sharing a piece of information with Burns and expecting him to follow through on it with finesse." He glanced at her, gaze bleak. "I discovered Mrs. Halliday's nephew, Jeffrey, ran an online porn site for pedophiles."

Laney's stomach turned. "You told Burns this?"

"Yes. That information alone was enough to charge the nephew with a crime. I figured the rest of the case would unravel from there, and the heat would come off Renee." He grimaced as if a sharp pain had struck him. "I was right, and I was so tragically wrong."

"Burns didn't follow up?"

Noah ran his fingers through his hair. "Like a bull in a china shop. That's his style."

"Don't I know it!"

"Jeffrey was indicted for the Web site, but he got out on bail. Can you believe it? The Hallidays refused to believe any relative of theirs would be involved in child pornography and put up the money." He shook his head.

"People never want to believe something terrible about someone they love."

Noah shot her a funny half smile, and Laney pruned her lips. He was still riding that tired old horse about her family having dirty laundry to hide.

She shifted in her seat. "So if the FBI finally had the right guy in their sights, what happened to put Renee in danger?"

Noah's expression went distant, his gaze fixed on the road. "She was going to be a key witness in the trial, so the nephew snatched her and ran."

Laney locked her fingers together. "This creep kidnapped your fiancée?"

"I traced them north to a secluded cabin on Lake Superior," Noah continued in the same dead tone, as if Laney hadn't spoken. "I thought I was making progress in talking him into letting Renee go if I allowed him to vanish into Canada, but about that time Burns and his team arrived with all their bells and whistles. Jeffrey lost it. He shot Renee and then himself. The FBI found the body of the kidnapped little girl under the floorboards of the cabin. Case closed, but an innocent woman was dead."

"Oh, Noah." Laney wrapped her hand around his arm. The muscles were tight as banjo strings. "I'm so sorry, but how could you think any of that was your fault?"

His glance shot fire. "Renee and I had plans to be together the evening Jeffrey took her, but I postponed our date on an excuse. While an evil man kidnapped her, I was out buying an engagement ring. If I'd been where I was supposed to be…" Noah didn't finish the thought.

The terrible injustice of those events set sharp claws into Laney's heart. "You couldn't have known, Noah." Sad empathy draped her words. She knew well the litany of what-ifs. "He would have chosen another time, or even killed you and taken her anyway."

A long breath gushed from Noah's lips. "I know that, but it doesn't stop me from wishing I could turn back time and make a different choice."

Laney barked a laugh. "I hear you."

A comradely silence fell. She could see now that Noah truly did understand how she felt about her negligence the day Gracie disappeared. Only he'd been doing something noble and good—buying an engagement ring for the love of his life. But she'd chosen selfish amusement over her own sister.

God judged the motives of the heart. Surely, He'd taken account of hers, and she'd fallen severely short. If she couldn't forgive herself, how could she expect Him to forgive her?

TWELVE

The next morning, Laney woke up in a lonely motel room. Yesterday's conversation with Noah hadn't done anything to perk up her spirits…or her hopes for getting to know him better. The guy still carried a torch for his lost love. How could she compete with this perfect ghost he held sacred in his heart?

The tasks that loomed before them today didn't cheer her, either. Going back to the old neighborhood and dredging up bad memories was her idea of torture. Noah had told her about the soil on the backpack coming from the Grand Valley area. That information pretty much confirmed that the pervert had to come back here to retrieve the backpack. If current suspects didn't pan out, Noah had hinted that one of their old neighbors could be responsible. The thought turned her stomach, but painful memories had to be faced, and questions needed to be asked.

Laney forced herself to get up and shuffle off to

the bathroom. Though she'd lived in this town for the first ten years of her life, she'd never been in Grand Valley's only lodging place. The amenities weren't five star, but the place was clean and well-maintained. Had Noah found out anything more about Richard Hodge? He'd said he was going to follow up on some ideas last night after they arrived and rented adjoining rooms. Noah had been impressively thorough at checking out her room's window and door locks. Then he left her inside and made sure she locked up tight before saying a muffled good-night through the door and heading to his room. Knowing he was near had helped her fall asleep last night, but it hadn't helped her stay asleep. Every little creak and groan had popped her eyes wide open. No wonder she was dragging today.

After she finished in the bathroom, Laney used her cell to call her folks in Louisville and got a good report that all was well there. Briana was sleeping in so Laney didn't get to talk to her. That was a disappointment, but at least her little princess was relaxed enough to slumber. She flipped her phone shut, and immediately the hotel phone shrilled. She hesitated with her hand over the receiver. It was probably Noah. She shoved the memory of that other nasty phone call to the back of her mind.

"Good morning!" Noah all right. "Where's a good place to eat around this burg? I'm starving."

Laney bit back a smart remark at his chipper morning manner. "If the Pantry Café still exists, that's probably where you'd like to go. They serve pancakes so huge they overlap the sides of the plate."

"Sounds like my kind of eating establishment. How soon will you be ready?"

"Give me fifteen minutes."

Twenty minutes later, they hopped into his vehicle and headed toward main street. A partly cloudy day muted the sunshine and reflected her mood.

Laney gazed around. "Oh, that gas station didn't used to be there." She looked some more. "And what happened to the Dairy Freeze? My friends and I used to ride our bikes to get the best dip cones there. Oh, man! The theater's closed, too. It's a second-hand store now."

Noah sent her a gentle smile. "Things change after eighteen years. Let's hope there hasn't been so much change that there's no trace left to point us to what really happened back then."

A cold shudder rippled through Laney. Yes, she wanted justice for Grace, and she and Briana needed to be safe, but what might they find along the route to that end? Did she really want to look into the face of this monster? *God, help me please.* From somewhere she needed to dredge up more courage than she felt right now.

"There it is!" she cried. "At least the Pantry is still here." They went inside and Laney laughed.

"This place is exactly as I remember it. Oh, maybe they've put down new carpet and painted the walls, but the tables and booths are right where they've always been."

Noah ushered her to a nearby booth. "As long as those pancakes are the same as you've described, I'll be a happy man." They took seats opposite each other as his head swiveled this way and that. "The joint is hopping."

"It always is this time of morning." Several tables were occupied by older men dressed in jeans or overalls and drinking coffee. Their hearty laughs rang out, along with the clatter of dice from the black cups at each table. "It's tradition," she told Noah. "They shake for who buys the java. Most of these guys are retired farmers. In about an hour, it'll be same song, second verse, only from an influx of businessmen wearing suits or sport shirts and dress pants."

A waitress in black slacks and a white pullover shirt came with menus, and they both ordered coffee to start off with.

"Do you recognize anyone?" Noah asked.

Laney scratched her brow. "A few faces look familiar, but I'm stumped on names."

Noah nodded. "Everyone is in groups or pairs and acting like they know other people."

Laney jerked her chin in the direction of a lone man taking a seat in a booth across the room. "What about him?"

"FBI. I picked up on him following us in his car this morning."

Laney wrinkled her nose. "How do you do that?"

"Practice." He flipped the menu open. "Now I'm going to relax and enjoy my breakfast."

They ordered their breakfasts, and when the cakes came, Noah's eyes widened. "You weren't kidding about their size."

"Did you think I was prone to small-town exaggeration?" Laney laughed. "Did you have any luck on your inquiries about Richard Hodge last night?"

Noah poured syrup over his steaming stack of cakes. "Mostly I sent off a series of e-mails from my laptop. His old employers weren't going to be in their offices that time of evening." He glanced up from his food project and a smile flickered in her direction. "I'll let you know what comes of my efforts."

"Mysterious man," she muttered and attacked her pancakes.

A half hour later, Noah drove them over to Laney's old neighborhood. She got out of the car and stood staring. The same homes she remembered still stood on either side of her block, but all but one sported either a fresh coat of paint or new siding.

Noah came up beside her. "Which one was yours?"

She pointed to a two-story, 1950s-era house

sitting in the center of the east side of the block. When they lived in it, the clapboard siding glowed with white paint. Now it was sided in dark tan vinyl, and the landscaping had changed. The sides and front of the house sported blooming bushes set in rocks. Her mother used to plant elaborate flower beds and care for them meticulously. Laney smiled at the memory of her mom, dressed in old shorts and a T-shirt, kneeling beside a flat of pansies, nestling the plants into place. Her family had been happy here, before… She swallowed, jerked thoroughly back to the present.

Laney touched Noah's arm and pointed to the house with peeling paint and unkempt yard next to her former home. "I wonder what happened to the Addison's home. They must have sold it to someone really low rent. George Addison and my dad used to have a friendly rivalry to see who had the greenest lawn and freshest paint."

Noah nodded. "We'll start on the side of the block opposite your old home. It's my pet theory that our perp revisited the scene of the crime in order to retrieve that backpack from wherever he stashed your sister. We want to know if anyone has observed a stranger in the area."

Forty-five minutes later, they'd spoken with about half the home owners, mostly retirees with the exception of a stay-at-home young mom. No one answered the door at the other houses. The owners were probably at work, so Noah said they'd have to come back in the evening to interview those households.

The nice people they encountered were only too willing to answer their questions, particularly when they found out that Laney was the little girl who used to live across the street. Only a few of the current residents were in place at the time of Grace's abduction and remembered her family, but sympathy made them accommodating anyway. The FBI had canvassed the area days ago, so everyone knew fresh incidents had reopened the old case. Unfortunately, nobody had noticed strangers lurking around or any unusual happenings in the neighborhood during the past couple of weeks.

Discouraged, Laney walked beside Noah up a cracked and frost-heaved sidewalk toward the dilapidated structure that used to house a family that the senior Thompsons considered their best friends. Laney hadn't particularly cared for the Addisons' boy, Watts, but then slightly older boys tended to feel superior and pick on younger girls. Quite possibly he'd grown into a fine man with the passage of time.

Noah led the way up the steps and knocked on the warped front door. Laney stood behind him and rubbed damp palms on her jeans. This place gave her the creeps, when it used to whisper welcome. No answer came from inside. Laney started to turn away, but Noah knocked again. A few moments later, the muffled clump of footfalls responded from inside.

The door creaked ajar and a scowling face peered out. A pair of bloodshot eyes glared at them above a flabby, bewhiskered jaw. "I've got no interest in what you're selling, especially if it's some flavor of religion."

Laney's heart rate kicked into overdrive. The face was nearly unrecognizable, but she knew that voice. Stepping forward, she held out her hand. "George Addison? Do you remember me? It's Laney. Laney Thompson. We're looking for information about—"

"How dare you come here?" George's face darkened, and a vein in his forehead bulged. Nasty whiskey breath blew into her nostrils. "Hasn't your family hurt mine enough?" He slammed the door in their faces.

"Who does that man think he is, talking about my family that way?" Laney sat poker-stiff in the passenger seat of the car as Noah drove away from her old neighborhood.

He'd be entertained at her outrage if the situation wasn't so serious. The gentle lady had a temper when aroused, and look out!—her family was sacred. After George Addison slammed the door, Laney was all for beating it down. He'd never seen her so worked up. But they didn't need an incident on their hands when their investigation in Grand

Valley was barely underway, so he escorted the fuming woman from the premises.

"Do you have any idea what Addison's outburst meant?" Noah ventured.

Laney crossed her arms. "Of course, I don't. Our family was never anything but good to his. Maybe he's mad because we stopped socializing after Grace was taken. Couldn't he be the least bit understanding?" She spread her hands. "We were hurting and didn't know who to trust."

Noah lifted his brows. "So you did suspect neighbors?"

Her face puckered. "Not the Addisons, really. We were too close with them. But, yes, when the investigation first got underway, the FBI talked pretty tough that the first place they look is a family member. The agents, especially Burns, grilled us like well-done steaks. And then when Mom, Dad and I were exonerated with airtight alibis, they started looking at people in the neighborhood. It wasn't until everyone in the area was extensively investigated that they concluded Grace's disappearance must be a case of stranger abduction."

Noah nodded. She'd grown calmer as she talked. "Don't you think we need to figure out why Mr. Addison has developed this animosity toward your family?"

"Well…sure." She shrugged. "But I don't see how that reason can connect with Grace's disappearance. As far as I know, when we moved from Grand Valley a few months later, we were still on good terms with the Addisons. They helped us pack."

"Did your family stay in touch with theirs?"

Laney fell silent. She twiddled her fingers against the car seat. "I—I don't think so. I never would have written or called their teenage son, but my folks never talked about George and Adelle again after we moved."

"Don't you think that's a little odd?"

She awarded him a steady stare. "Not really. We were trying to put everything about Grand Valley behind us. Avoiding any mention of that place was the only way we could cope with the pain."

Noah nodded. "I can understand that." He turned into the motel parking lot. "I want to check my e-mail, then you can tell me about your former good friends."

He booted his computer up in the motel office while Laney got a couple of bottles of juice from a vending machine. She'd said her family was close with the Addisons', but from the way she talked about the son, it was more the parents who were close than the whole family. It would be interesting to explore the dynamics of that relationship. Depending on what they discovered as the reason behind George Addison's animosity, he might have to talk to Roland and Loretta about their former neighbors.

Laney handed him a bottle of juice, and he thanked her. She settled into a guest chair opposite him and pulled out her cell phone. "I haven't talked to Briana yet today."

His e-mail came up. Richard Hodge's former employers from different communities had responded to his inquiry. Hodge had worked as custodian at a manufacturing plant, then in an office building, then in a nursing home before landing at the school in Cottonwood Grove. The answers from the manufacturing plant and the office building were disappointing—no known physical handicap or problems in his feet. Their responses to his repeated question about reason for leaving employment continued to be vague—relocation.

Noah frowned. There had to be a reason why a young, healthy guy moved from town to town and job to job. He'd thought about that when he hired the man, but Hodge had the most custodial experience, with well-rounded skills in trouble-shooting electrical and plumbing issues, of any of the applicants. Noah clicked on the third e-mail. It was longer than the others. Maybe there'd be some meat here. He'd barely started reading, when Laney thrust her phone at him.

"Bree wants to talk to you," she said.

He blinked, pulling himself out of investigator mode. "Okay." He took the cell. "Hi, princess."

A giggle answered him. "Mama says she can't wait to get home and see me. You, too?"

"My day is always brighter when I can see you." The words came out with his whole heart in them. This mother and daughter owned him in ways Renee hadn't even touched. He hadn't known it was possible to feel this strongly about anyone, but he couldn't explore those feelings…yet. "What are you up to today?" He kept his tone light.

"Not much. Grandpa says we're going to stick around home, but Grandma says that's okay because she needs help baking cookies."

Noah laughed. "Wish I was there to help you eat them."

"I'll save you one for when you bring Mama home." The little voice oozed confidence. "I been praying, and God promised me something." Her volume eased down to a whisper. "But I'm not supposed to tell yet."

Noah's stomach tightened. What was the child talking about? Had she remembered something about the day the backpack was left? "If it's about the bad man, you need to tell."

"Nope. Not about him. And I'm not telling."

Noah shook his head. Evidently, the sweet little girl shared a stubborn streak with her sweet little mother. If it turned out he had a chance to win Laney's heart, he'd have to get used to that. He chuckled. "Enjoy your cookies, princess."

They closed the call, and he gave the phone back to Laney, who was grinning at him. "She can be a handful when she wants to be."

"Normal little girl." He returned to his e-mail while Laney sipped her juice.

Noah hissed in a breath. "I think we have a winner here."

She straightened. "Hodge has foot problems?"

"No, he has a learning disability. He's dyslexic."

"Really?" Her eyes bugged. "I never would have guessed."

"I have a hunch this may be the key to discovering what motivated him to flood the school."

Laney's brow puckered. "But how could this guy's struggles with dyslexia relate to Grace's disappearance?"

Noah regarded her soberly. "It may not, but we'll see. This employer has graciously included Richard's mother's address. They did a recheck of his file and found it on a slip of paper crumpled up in the fold. Evidently, that's the address where they sent his final paycheck. I'm going to pass this information on to Hank. Who knows? They may even find the guy holed up at Mommy's house."

She beamed at him. "Now, that's progress."

Noah forwarded the e-mail from Hodge's former employer to the sheriff, along with a brief update on his and Laney's activities. Then he shut down his computer.

He picked up his full juice bottle. "Now we need to make progress on the mystery of George Addison."

His investigator sense said that they'd stumbled

on to a significant lead, but Laney might hate where the trail took them. Something had gone on between the Thompsons and the Addisons that wasn't right.

THIRTEEN

Laney polished off her juice, then got up and tossed the plastic container in the recycle bin. She'd humor Noah with this line of questioning, but she liked the lead on Richard Hodge much better.

"Mr. Addison is a building contractor," she said. "When our families lived next door, he was successful at it. Doesn't look like he is anymore."

"A drinking problem will do that to people." Noah frowned.

"I suspect Adelle has left him, or the place wouldn't have gone to seed like that. She was a fussy woman, always nagging him about one task or another."

Noah nodded. "The question is whether the drinking problem drove the wife away, or if the wife leaving brought out the drunk in him. Or maybe it was something else."

Laney caught her breath. "Like guilt over killing a little girl?"

"Maybe."

She perked up on a thought. "I know someone who may be able to give us the inside scoop about what happened with the Addisons…if he's still alive, and if that little body shop and gas station still exists on the far end of town."

"Let's go." Noah led the way out to the car.

Laney buckled her seat belt as long-suppressed memories flooded to the surface. "Our families used to have cookouts together at least once a week. Our dads were on the same bowling league, and our moms belonged to the same horticulture society. Plus, we'd go camping together at least once in the summertime over at Forestville State Park not far from here. There's a great big cave there. A tourist attraction." She gasped. "Do you think that's where—"

"No, too well-trafficked." Noah shook his head. "Was Watts a good playmate?"

"At times." She grimaced. "But more often he'd tease Grace and me when the adults weren't around. I guess that's not surprising behavior for a young boy. When we first got to know the Addisons, Watts was at the age where girls had cooties. By the time we moved away, he was fourteen years old and starting to change his tune about the opposite sex. But a gangly ten-year-old and a mentally challenged eight-year-old were nuisances, not attractions."

Noah chuckled. "I can relate. I was that age once. No doubt you stood up for yourself just fine, but how did you feel about him teasing Grace?"

She laughed. "I gave him a black eye once." She whooshed her fist through the air, remembered exhilaration tingling her flesh.

Noah hooted. "I would have liked to be a fly on the wall to see that."

"It was a sneak shot." She wrinkled her nose. "He was too much bigger than me for the punch to be anything else."

Noah glanced at her, face dark. "Did he hit back?"

"If I recall correctly, he ran off wailing with his hand over his face. He left Grace and me alone from then on. But he may have told his mother what happened. She never liked me after that. Turn here," she added quickly, and Noah barely made the corner at an intersection between two highways. "Sorry about that." She sent him an apologetic look. "Oh, there it is."

Squat and square and painted white, the body shop and gas station looked exactly as she remembered it, as if time had stood still on this little speck of earth. Noah pulled into the parking lot. A pair of pumps sat outside a small office area, and side-by-side garage stalls stood open with vehicles in various stages of body work parked inside. Beside the office door, a wizened figure perched on a stool, nursing a bottle of Pepsi.

Laney chuckled. "I can hardly believe he's still here. This guy is a town institution. He doesn't own the place. He's not even related to the owner, but he might as well have a lease on that spot he sits every day. Let me introduce you." She got out of the car, and Noah followed.

"I can hardly wait for this," he said with a chuckle.

The man on the stool regarded their approach with a crinkly faced smile. He'd lost another tooth up front since Laney last saw him. They stopped shy of the single step up to the office entrance.

"Mr. Bingham, do you remember me?"

The elderly gentleman rested his bottle on his knee and squinted at her with faded gray eyes. "You've got the look of someone…" His lips bunched together and then released in a gap-toothed grin. "It can't be! Loretta Thompson's little girl all grown up as pretty as her mother."

Her face warmed. "Yes, it's me, Laney. I'd like to introduce you to my friend, Noah."

Noah shook the other man's hand. "Hello, Mr. Bingham. We're looking into Grace Thompson's disappearance. Laney says you're the man to see about some questions we have."

"Call me Bing," the old gentleman said. "Everybody does. And Laney's right. There's not much goes on in this burg that doesn't reach my ears." He tugged one lobe. "If I don't know a thing, it ain't worth knowin'."

They joined Bing in a round of laughter, but Laney couldn't sustain the merriment. Too much weighed on her heart.

"We visited Laney's old neighborhood," Noah said, "and had a run-in with George Addison."

Good humor faded from Bing's expression. "Sad case."

Laney put one foot on the step and leaned toward the old man. "What happened to the Addisons?"

Bing's gray gaze went veiled beneath thick lashes any woman would envy. A tremor ran through Laney's bones. Why did she get the feeling the old man pitied her? He took a slurp from his pop bottle, and glanced up at Noah, who'd gone still as a hunter awaiting his prey. What did he expect to hear? Why did a part of her not want to listen?

The elderly man returned his attention to Laney. "George and Adelle split up shortly after you folks moved away. Adelle took Watts and left town. Never came back. George went into a tailspin. In and out of jail with DUIs. He's lost his license several times. Next time, they won't give it back. Within a few years, his contractor business went down the tubes. Now he barely makes ends meet doing odd jobs. That is, when he can pry himself out of Bucky's Bar."

"Any idea why Adelle Watts divorced her husband?" Noah pressed.

Bing studied his Pepsi label. "That woman never was content. Rode George something fierce."

"So the marriage was unhappy?" Laney burst out. "I had a feeling, even as a kid."

The man nodded his head. "Kids see things. They know things." His gaze spoke volumes Laney didn't understand.

Noah stepped forward. "But what was the catalyst that spurred the breakup?"

"Hard to say. Expect you'd have to ask George about that." Bing polished off his Pepsi and held out the empty container to Noah. "Spot an old geezer for another one?"

"Happy to." Noah grinned and pulled a fist full of change from his pocket. "You've been very helpful."

Laney shifted her weight from one foot to another. "But—"

Noah's warm fingers closed around her elbow, and he drew her toward his car. She shot him a disgusted look. Couldn't he see Bing was holding back? Noah winked at her, and she subsided in his grasp. Either the man had another plan, or he'd decided the Addisons' problems had nothing to do with Grace's disappearance. Either way was fine with her. She didn't want to know any more about George and Adelle's dirty laundry.

"What next?" she asked as she settled into the vehicle.

"We're going to grab lunch, and then you're going to take me to the spot where Grace's blood was found."

Laney's throat thickened. There's no way she could choke down a bite with that prospect ahead of her.

* * *

An hour and a half later found them pulling into an approach next to a wooded area along a gravel road about a mile out of town. Noah parked the car and looked over at his passenger. Laney's face had pulled tight into a white-washed mask.

He touched her small hand balled in a fist on the seat next to him. "Did you ever come out here after the last trace of your sister was found in the ravine?"

She shook her head. "This area was a wonderland of adventure for the local kids when I was growing up. After Grace, I tried to come here a couple of times, but got no farther than this before a panic attack would set in, and I had to turn my bike around or pass out. I've imagined it plenty in my mind, though, and had nightmares. All the blood…" She bit her lower lip.

Noah's heart twisted. He hated doing this to her, but he needed to see the spot. Sometimes looking at a place where a crime occurred sparked ideas about how it might have happened, which could even hint at who did it. And maybe Laney revisiting this place in its natural, pristine state would help her lay ghosts of her imagination to rest.

Noah took her hand. "You said there were caves in the area, right?"

She nodded wordlessly, gaze fixed on a faint trail that led between maples, aspens and pines. Noah tugged her with him into the trees. A whip-poor-will called, and a lively breeze set the leaves to whispering. This was a romantic setting, not a scary one…to him maybe. Laney's hand stayed stiff as a board in his. They passed down and up several hollows. Then a crack in the earth yawned to their left.

"Here." Laney stopped. "They found her blood at the bottom of the ravine where it first skirts the trail. I heard the sheriff tell my parents that."

Noah peered over the edge. The weed-grown incline was too steep and rocky to navigate at this point, but several yards away the slope gentled. "We're going down."

Laney pulled her hand away and hugged herself. "I'll stay here and wait for you."

Noah shook his head. "I can't leave you alone. I'm not merely your investigator. I'm your bodyguard. Remember?"

Her haunted blue eyes begged for a different answer. "My heart is nearly pounding out of my chest."

Noah laid his hands on her shoulders. "I'll be with you every second. You need to see there's nothing down there."

Deep breaths quavered in and out of her lungs. "I know you're right, but I don't think I can do it."

"I have faith in your courage."

He took her hand again and guided the way. Step by careful step they eased downward. Rocks and pebbles disturbed by their feet plinked ahead of them. A creek had once run here, but the water was long dried up, and weeds had grown over the streambed. Weathered stones and boulders protruded from the soil.

"Are any of the caves down here?"

"No-o." Laney's voice cracked. She cleared her throat. "Those are farther up the trail."

They reached the bottom, and Laney stood riveted, staring around with enormous eyes. Noah's gaze took in the area. The ravine was about twenty feet across at the top and several feet wide at the base. The crack in the earth extended as far as the eye could see in either direction, most of it fairly sheer. Noah looked up the way they'd come. Grace's abductor would have needed to be nimble and strong to carry her down, especially if she were struggling. Unless—his gaze narrowed on the steep drop into the ravine where the child's blood had been found.

"There's nothing here." Laney's tone was filled with wonder. The harshness of her breathing had eased. "I mean, I knew we wouldn't see any trace of Gracie after all this time, but I always thought that if I came here I'd feel her spirit…accusing me."

"And you don't."

Her gaze found his. "If anything, I feel peace."

Noah smiled and squeezed her hand. He let go and felt her following him as he moved closer to the spot the child must have met her end. The area was strewn with boulders, any one of which could crack a skull like an egg.

"Maybe she wasn't carried down here but fell."

"A fall here could easily kill anyone." Laney came up beside him. "It's a wonder one of us hooligan kids tearing around out here didn't take a tumble. But how did my sister get out to this area in the first place?"

"We're not that far from town. Could she have decided to take a walk? Maybe she got here and someone chased her."

"Or she thought someone was chasing her. Gracie could be skittish that way."

Noah rubbed his chin. "But someone carted her body away."

"Exactly. And another thing, Grace would never, ever have wandered away on her own. That's why I was so confident she would go straight home after I got her onto our block where she could see our house. Autistics are very much creatures of habit. She wouldn't have gone exploring by herself."

He planted his hands on his hips. "So someone brought her out here. But she could have escaped and ran, then fell into the ravine."

"That's a good theory."

"But without proof it's nothing more. Finding Grace's body could provide that proof. Let's go see those caves."

Laney led the way up onto the path, confidence

restored to her step. Within several hundred yards they came to the end of the ravine. Soon they stepped out of the trees into a vast clearing. Ahead, the horizon was ragged with low cliffs.

"There are half a dozen caves in those rocks." Laney pointed toward them. "But they're small and have been played in by local kids before and after Grace's death."

"It can't hurt to look again."

She shrugged.

The sun bathed them in hot rays as they crossed the expanse of meadow dotted with white and yellow wild flowers. As they drew close, Noah estimated the cliffs were only about fifty or sixty feet high. Shallow cracks and fissures showed here and there, and a narrow skirt of sloped rock offered access to higher elevations.

Noah's cell phone sounded, and he pulled it from his belt holder. "Just a second, Laney. It's Hank."

She waved and stopped. He flipped his cell open.

"Ryder here."

"We got Hodge."

"With his mother?"

"Nope." The man chuckled. "But finding her led to finding the kid brother, and bingo!"

"What's our man got to say for himself?" Noah did a slow turn, surveying the area.

"He's carping about how everyone picked on

him at school growing up. He's especially angry that he was shunted into special education classes that never did him any good."

"So the guy did have it in for Laney." He continued his slow swivel.

"Not her, per se. What she stood for. But he's blank as a slate when we ask him anything about Grand Valley and a little girl that disappeared eighteen years ago. Claims he was a circus roustabout on the west coast at the time, but that's a job he never put on his résumé."

"Have you been able to check the story out?"

"Yep. And he's telling the truth. This guy sabotaged the school all right, but he didn't kidnap Laney's little sister."

Noah huffed a breath. "She'll be disappointed. She had high hopes about Hodge as a suspect, but I had my doubts. Any sign of Glen Crocker yet?"

"Negative. If he's our guy, you might want to watch for him where you're at."

"I'm checking right now for any tail Laney and I might have acquired."

Had he seen movement among the trees? His muscles tensed, and his gaze zeroed in on the spot. Could be their FBI tail. Nope. Just a clump of ferns waving at him. Unease filtered through him. Was this guy going to make another try for Laney? Or was some other nasty plan in the works?

"Do me a favor, Hank. I have to get a guy to talk to me tonight, and I think we're running out of time

to close this case before a fresh tragedy happens."
Noah told the sheriff what he wanted, and they
ended the call.

He slapped his phone shut and turned toward
Laney, but blank cliff face met his gaze. His
stomach twisted into a knot in his throat. This
couldn't be happening again! A brief moment of
inattention, and the woman he loved was gone.

FOURTEEN

"Laneeeey!"

Noah's panicked cry stood the hair straight up on the back of her neck. She raced out of the tiny cave so familiar from her childhood days of carefree exploration and hopped from rock to rock downward. The lone figure in the meadow below whipped around one direction then another, frantically calling.

"I'm here," she cried, stopping on a rock above his head.

He whirled toward her voice, face gray as a corpse. "Laney," he breathed. Color rushed into his cheeks.

"I'm sorry, Noah. I didn't think." She took a step. "I—" Her foot slipped, and she screamed as she tumbled toward the ground.

Noah cried her name again, and his strong frame broke her fall. A moment later, Laney found earth beneath her feet and solid arms around her, squeezing the breath from her body. She gazed up into green eyes fierce with—what? Fear? Fury? Both? And maybe something else.

"Never scare me like that again." His voice rasped, and his lips found hers.

The kiss was deep and long and strong. Not the wild, demanding kind she'd at first thought so exciting from Clayton, but later learned was all take and no give. Noah's kiss, like his embrace, was steady and solid from the sort of man who knew the meaning of commitment. Laney's heart soared as she wrapped her arms around his neck.

Noah pulled back first and rested his chin on the top of her head. "Now what am I going to do with you, Laney Thompson?"

"I like this fine," she said into his shirt.

A brief chuckle rumbled in her ear. "No, I mean now that I've gone against every promise I've made myself and fallen top over tail for a woman who's my client, where can you stay that you'll be safe until this case is solved? I suppose the FBI would put you in protective custody." He held her away from him, and Laney felt bereft of his closeness. "This moment has made me realize that I can't protect you and do my job at the same time…just as I feared."

She gazed into his troubled face. "You're thinking wrong, Noah. Being here is my choice. You can't control that, and I don't expect you to protect me. Sometimes safety is overrated when the stakes are this high."

Noah chucked her under the chin. "Sell your father that line."

She smiled and ran the pads of her fingers down his lean cheek. "My father is being a father, and you're being wonderful you—the man who wants to cocoon the world in his cupped hands. I've heard tell that's God's job."

He turned his head and planted a kiss in her palm. A delicious shiver ran down her spine.

Laney pulled her hand away. "Don't distract me from my lecture." She shook a finger at him. "Here, you let me think all this time that you weren't the least bit interested."

"Considering all the people who saw through me, I'm amazed I fooled you."

"And who was that?"

"Miss Aggie, for one. And your mom, who told your dad."

Her face warmed, and she looked away. "I'm a little insecure about my judgment concerning men, so I did my best to respect what I thought were your wishes and behave businesslike around you. My mom saw through me, too."

"Well, I didn't. I was desperately hoping that I might have a chance with you after this mess was sorted out, but I wasn't sure about that, what with Pierce Mayfield hanging around."

"Oh, him." Laney scrunched up her nose. "He seems gallant and good-natured, but he doesn't make my heart do somersaults with his smile."

"Somersaults? Really?" He grinned like a kid, and she could swear his chest expanded. Then he sobered. "So what about that FBI protective custody?"

"Forget it." She sliced the air with her hands.

He sighed. "Then whatever you do, do not get out of my sight, unless I leave you somewhere behind locked doors."

"I can live with that."

"Then let's go explore those caves…together."

This adorable woman's stubborn streak was going to drive him straight up the wall. "You don't have to sit up until one o'clock and go on this little foray with me," he told Laney during a leisurely supper at a chain restaurant next to the motel.

The inspection of the caves had turned up nothing. They were little more than holes in the cliff wall. Wildlife wouldn't even consider them decent dens, and certainly no place to hide a body. Besides, that backpack had been kept somewhere enclosed. Maybe a cave wasn't the place at all. Then where? They'd also finished canvassing her neighborhood, with no result.

Noah mentally shook his head. This gambit tonight had better strike pay dirt, but he wasn't sure he wanted Laney anywhere near George Addison. The man had acted scary ugly when they showed up on his doorstep.

"I am not afraid of the town drunk," Laney told

him. "Though, I'm a little afraid of the slander he might spew about my family. Something had to make him so mad, even if it's a figment of his sauced imagination. But I do need to hear what he's got to say."

Noah capitulated with upraised hands. "Let me handle the guy. You keep quiet, or you could set him off raving, and we won't get a lick of sense out of him."

"I'll do my best."

Noah read sincerity in her expression, but he knew her knee-jerk reactions when it came to anyone maligning her family. She might not be able to help herself. *Whoo-ee!* They could be in for an interesting ride.

He paid for their meal, and they walked across the asphalt toward their motel. Noah's gaze ranged over the area. The highway ran to their left, and traffic was sporadic. No vehicles slowed and none in the parking areas looked out of place or held anyone sitting and staring—other than the FBI guy. To their right, beyond the buildings, lay a corn field with green stalks about a foot above the ground. No place for a watcher to hide there, either.

Laney touched the back of his hand. "My ever-vigilant protector."

He smiled down into her glowing face, and their fingers entwined. Alarm bells clamored in the back of his mind, but there was no taking back the kiss in the meadow, even if he wanted to put a recall on it. Which he didn't.

"We need to try to take a nap now," he told Laney as they reached their rooms. "We could be up all hours of the night."

"Just a second." She tugged him to a stop near a bench outside the rooms. "I want to call Mom and Dad and update them." She pulled a cell phone from her purse and sat down.

"Okay." Noah tucked his hands into his jeans pockets.

What would she tell her folks about this sudden development in their relationship? Or maybe it wasn't sudden. Comparing notes over supper, they'd discovered they had been fighting mutual attraction since he'd first interviewed her for the job at the school. He frowned. This wasn't exactly the time he would have chosen to make his move, but emotion had overridden judgment. And that's what he'd feared about taking on a client that stirred his heart.

Maybe he should remove himself from the case. But where would that leave Laney and little Briana? In a worse spot than with him on it. He was caught between the proverbial rock and a hard place.

"Hi, Mom," Laney said into the phone.

From her end of the conversation, Noah gathered that Roland was out, and Loretta and Briana were home in the company of one of the private guards Roland had hired. Laney told her mother about their trip to the site where the last sign of Grace had been found, but she didn't mention the kiss in the meadow. Noah mentally mopped his forehead. It was better if her folks didn't know they'd made a giant leap in their relationship a bit prematurely. Then she told her mother about canvassing the old neighborhood. Loretta must have had a lot of questions about that because Laney kept stopping and explaining details. Then she got to George Addison.

"The guy was a total wreck, Mom. You wouldn't believe it if you saw him. And bitter, too. We had a visit with old Mr. Bingham down at the station afterward. He says Adelle and Watts left him shortly after we moved away."

Noah couldn't hear the response from the other end, but Laney's posture stiffened.

"Okay," she finally said, then paused. "Sure, put her on."

The next few minutes passed with Laney chatting with her daughter. Then she held the phone up to him, grinning. "She wants to talk to you, too."

Noah took the phone and visited with the little princess about the cookie she was saving for him and the bedtime story she expected him to read to her next time they were together. The child's steady faith that he was supposed to be a fixture in her life amazed and encouraged him. Maybe everything would work out all right.

"Tell Mama I'll say special prayers for you and her tonight," Briana said.

"That would be much appreciated," Noah told her. And for some reason, assurance of her simple faith lightened the load of questions and uncertainties in his mind.

They finished the conversation, and Noah held the phone toward Laney. "What's the matter?"

She was sitting with her hands on her knees and a dark frown on her face. "I don't know. Something. Mom was so upset to hear that the Addisons' marriage failed and George has become an alcoholic that I didn't have the heart to tell her that we're going to talk to him again tonight. In fact, she ordered me to stay away from him."

"Maybe you should rethink coming with me."

Her jaw firmed, and she stood up. "Let's grab that nap. Who knows what kind of a night is ahead of us."

At ten after one of a moonlit morning, Noah stood outside Bucky's Bar and waited while stragglers exited. He'd left Laney sitting in the backseat of his car in the parking lot. He checked the vehicle again. No one approached where it sat under a streetlight. This investigating and bodyguarding at the same time was more than he'd bargained for. But then, so was her warm response in his arms at the cave site. A smile grew on his face. One sick animal to put behind bars, and then he'd sentence himself to the gentlemanly courtship she deserved.

A grunt brought his head around. The pudgy figure of George Addison plodded out the bar's front door. The man went still, swaying from side to side and squinting at the handful of vehicles remaining in the parking lot. He paid no attention to Noah.

Noah took a step closer, and the fumes flowing from Addison nearly staggered him. "Do you plan on driving home?"

The man jumped and tipped backward, hitting the bar door with a thud. "Wha? Wha?" Bleary eyes blinked in Noah's direction. "Who are you?"

Noah grimaced. His target was nearly too far gone to walk, but he'd better not be too far gone to talk. "We met on the front step of your house today."

George let out a thick snort. "Yeah. You're the guy looking into Grashie's dishappearance." He nodded ponderously like a pickled sage. "I know 'cuz itsh all over town what you're up to."

The man heaved himself forward and began to cross the parking lot toward a dilapidated pickup.

Noah trailed him. "I'd like to ask you a few questions."

George waved a vague paw and continued his erratic course. "I don' know nothin'…" He belched. "'Bout that little girl."

Assaulted by fumes, Noah fell back. Then he

caught up with the guy as he patted himself all over and finally pulled keys from the front right pocket of his jeans.

Noah planted a hand against the pickup door. "If you attempt to drive yourself away in this vehicle, you'll be arrested and lose your license for good."

The man scowled at him. "How d'you know?"

Noah waved his arm in the air, and a darkened sedan across the street suddenly lit with red bubbles and bleeped a short wail. Hank had done that favor Noah asked him and encouraged the Grand Valley PD to help his plan out.

George's jaw hung slack, then he snapped it shut. "How'm I shposed to get home?"

"Let me drive you."

Laney's former neighbor gaped at the cop car, then looked at his own vehicle, and then at the keys in his hand. "You don' give a guy much choice."

Noah heaved an inward sigh of relief. With that much reasoning power left in his fogged brain, there was hope the man could supply useful information. And yet he was soused enough that, if he was Grace's killer, he might incriminate himself without realizing what he'd said.

Taking George by the elbow, Noah guided the man toward his car and helped him get in, police-style, without bumping his head. Then he hustled around to the driver's side. Laney didn't need to be alone with her former neighbor one second longer than necessary. She'd promised to be quiet and let him handle the interview, but her emotions were bubbling high after that conversation with her mother.

He settled behind the wheel and headed the car out of the parking lot. The vehicle reeked of cheap booze from the man sitting next to him, but Laney was keeping her part of the bargain…so far. If he hadn't seen her sitting primly in the back when he climbed in, he might wonder if she was still there.

George's head lolled against the seat rest.

"Stay awake and pay attention!" Noah nudged the man and received a glare for his troubles.

"What you wan' from me?"

"Why don't you start by telling me why you're so angry with a family of people who were once your best friends? After they lost a daughter so tragically, I'd think you'd have sympathy."

George gave a low growl. "I'm real sorry 'bout that li'l girl. She wash a funny thing, but I wished no bad on her. No, sirree. Not like that Jezebel of a mom of hers."

"My mother? What are you talking about?" Laney's demand cracked through the air, and Noah shot her a fierce look across his shoulder. Passing streetlights revealed she didn't have a glance to spare him. She stared at George Addison, who swiveled and squinted at her in return.

A mean smirk formed on his features. "You may ash well know, girlie. Maybe I'll feel better if I can wreck her family like she wrecked mine." His face twisted into a mask of fury. "Working out in the flower beds, bending over in them shorts. Drive a man inshane, I tell you!"

"Don't you dare talk about my mother that way!" Laney's palms smacked the back of his seat.

From her tone, Noah was surprised George had any eyeballs left in his head. Maybe he should call a halt to the hostilities. He hesitated and turned a corner. Then again, maybe the heat of this exchange would bring out the truth. What had the mystery phone caller said to Laney in the hospital? Something about making players pay? Now here was George reveling in causing trouble for Laney's family.

"She made me fall in love with her," George hissed. "I thought she loved me, too. Then she left me."

Laney leaned forward. Her white face and bared teeth loomed large in the rearview mirror. Noah caught his breath.

"There is no way my mother had an affair with the likes of you."

George's cold laugh shivered Noah's spine. "Why don't you ask her about that?" He rubbed a hand over his whiskery jowl. "I washn't hard to look at myself...back then. And that bumbling bear of a Roland didn' know the gem he had. All he did was work, work, work. Had no idea how to shatisfy a fine woman like that."

"No!" Laney's shout reverberated through the car.

Noah's heart went out to her but he couldn't shield her from this revelation.

"I won't listen to this." She slapped George's headrest, and the guy didn't even duck. Too snockered to appreciate his danger. "You're a liar! Are you a killer, as well? Did you kill my little sister?" She half lunged across the seat and grabbed George's collar.

Noah hastily pulled the car over to the curb, turned, and disengaged her fingers. Laney's frantic gaze stabbed hot shards of anguish through Noah.

He kept his grip around her wrists firm but gentle. "It's time for this to come out. Don't you see? We're unlocking a door that may show us what really happened to your sister and lead us to the person who threatens you and your daughter now."

Laney sobbed and wrenched her hands away, then fell back against her seat.

George fumbled with the door handle. "I don' gotta shtay in here with no crazy woman and some guy who's tryin' to shay I killed a kid."

Noah set a hand on the man's shoulder. "Where are your wife and son now?"

George went still. Then his whole body slumped. "You Thompsons think you're the only ones to lose a child. Adelle found out about the affair after your family left town. She took my boy." A whimper finished the sentence.

"Where?" Noah persisted. "Where did they go?"

An exaggerated shrug answered. "Don' know where Adelle is, but Watts is dead."

A gasp erupted from the backseat.

Noah's breath caught. "Your son is dead? Where did you attend the funeral?"

George snorted. "Not welcome at the funeral. Adelle shent me his obituary from the newshpaper, his death certificate and the urn with his ashes. Her brand of kindness." The man gave a blubbery snicker. "Showed them FBI agents that shtuff, when they came sniffin' around, wonderin' why I dove into the bottle." He nodded ponderously. "With no dad around to guide my boy, he turned into a wild teen. Got high one night and wrapped his car around a tree-ee." The last word broke in half as the man began to wail in earnest. Great wet gasps heaved from his chest. "A-and it's all because of what we done…m-me and Loretta."

Laney's sobs melded with George's.

Noah hung his head.

FIFTEEN

"I don't know who I hate more," Laney spat toward Noah, her stomach in a thousand knots. "George Addison, my mother…or you!"

"Me?" Noah rocked back.

They stood in the darkness outside her motel room door.

"It was your bright idea to go see George again." Laney knew her words were unfair even as they sprang from her mouth. She waved a hand between her and Noah. "I don't mean that. I don't know what I mean." Her fingernails chewed her palms. "I'm angry and I want to hit somebody, and you're close."

Noah scooped up her fisted hands and pressed them between his palms. "I'm sorry. I should have insisted you stay behind tonight."

"And then what would you have said to me after you found out all this from good old George?" She tugged her hands away and clutched her arms around herself. The evening breeze was cool, but her shiver didn't come from chill. "It's better that I heard this straight from the adulterer's mouth."

Noah frowned. "Are you going to call your mom?"

"No! Yes." Her breath came in ragged gulps. "No, I can't. First of all, I'm afraid of exactly what I might call her. Second, I can't talk to her on the phone about this. I need to see her face, look her in the eye. Third, what if my father answers the phone? He'll know instantly by my voice that I'm beside myself. I can't risk him finding out what Mom did to him—to all of us." A bile-tasting sob spurted between her lips. "But how am I going to live with this knowledge all alone?"

"You're not alone." Noah wrapped his arms around her.

She wilted in his embrace, but the real tears remained dammed behind a wall of outrage and disbelief. What could her mother have been thinking?

"How do you know your dad doesn't know?"

Noah's words passed through Laney's ears but went unregistered for several heartbeats. Then Laney gasped and pulled away.

She stared up into Noah's moon-shadowed face. "If my dad knew, it would have wrecked my parents' marriage the same as it did the Addisons'."

"Maybe."

She planted her hands on her hips. "Do you really think a marriage could withstand the loss of a daughter *and* the shattering of marriage vows?"

Noah's fingertips brushed across her forehead and tucked a strand of hair behind one ear. "I'm just saying there's a whole other side to this story that we haven't heard yet. Maybe things didn't happen exactly like George said."

A bitter laugh tainted Laney's mouth. "Funny to hear you defending my family when I've been the fanatic up to this point. I'm so stunned. I—I can't think straight. I think I'd like to be alone for a while." She pressed fingertips to her temple.

"Sure. I've got work to do anyway."

"This time of night?" Laney retrieved her room key from her purse.

"If Adelle Addison is out there somewhere nursing a grudge half the size of her ex-husband's, I need to find her fast."

"What about George? He could be the sick pervert who's doing all this."

Noah frowned. "Can you really see that wreck of a man planning and carrying out the kind of taunting that's being done to you?"

Laney didn't respond. The answer was self-evident. George wasn't a good candidate.

"I'll thoroughly vet George, too," Noah went on. "Find out what kind of alibi, if any, he had for the time of Gracie's death and for the days when evil pranks were played on you."

"Thanks, Noah. I'd be a raving lunatic right now if not for you. I mean that." If he could feel the waves of gratitude flowing out of her, he'd be bowled over.

"You're welcome." He leaned in and kissed her forehead. "Try to get some rest. Maybe things will look better in the morning."

"Sure," she said as she inserted the key in the lock. But with every stone they turned, more ugliness oozed out. How could things be right in her world ever again?

Inside her hotel room, Laney locked the doors and assured Noah she was bolted in. Next she switched on the bedside lamp and put her pajamas on. Then she paced. Physical exhaustion drew her toward the bed, but rest was far from her mind and emotions.

She'd lost her little sister. And now she'd lost her mother just as cruelly and completely. But at least this time the devastation wasn't her fault.

How could she not have noticed something going on between her mom and George Addison? Sure, there were times she'd seen that there was distance between her parents, but there'd been no fighting. Nothing to indicate their marriage was so sour that one of them might look elsewhere for love.

Could it even be called love when an adulterous couple got together? Where did they hold their secret trysts? When?

Her mom hadn't worked outside the home. Dad worked hard as a top insurance agent and brought in enough money to support the family. That way Mom could be home when Laney and Grace were little, which was especially important with a special needs child.

Of course, Mom would have had more free time after she and Grace were both in school, but George Addison had a thriving building contractor business. Especially in the summertime, he was gone from dawn until dusk, even more absent than Laney's father. George and her mom must have been extremely clever and creative—not to mention driven and obsessed—to risk so much on a fling.

Laney flopped onto the coverlet of the bed and lay with her arm across her face. A sudden jangling brought her bolt upright. Bleary-eyed, she checked the time on the bedside clock as the phone rang a second time.

5:30 a.m.

Who would be calling at this hour? Noah? Another taunting call?

Gingerly, she picked up the handset. "Hello?"

"Laney-girl?"

"Dad! Is something wrong? Is Bree—"

"The little princess is fine." Her dad's voice came across strong and calm.

Laney swallowed her heart back into place. "Why are you calling so early?"

"It's six-thirty here, but I couldn't wait any longer in case you and Noah got busy early today."

A sour taste rose from Laney's throat. They'd been investigating early all right, but she didn't dare mention anything to Dad about last night's bomb that blew up her life.

"Your mother told me you had a run-in with George Addison yesterday." He clucked his tongue. "We were hoping they'd moved from the area by now, and you wouldn't cross paths with the Addisons."

"What are you saying?" Laney rubbed a suddenly clammy hand against her pajama pants.

A deep sigh answered her. "Your mom and I are devastated about what happened to their family. We had no idea. We were up most of the night discussing what we need to do about it."

"Do about it?" Laney echoed. How did Mom and Dad propose to fix a friend's marriage that one of them had helped destroy?

"What we needed to do as far as *you're* concerned," Dad hastily clarified. "We decided we should to be the ones to tell you before you contact George again, and he spills the beans."

Laney's pulse stalled. Her dad knew!

"I'm afraid you're too late." Her voice rasped through a tight throat. "How…could…she?" Every word carried the force of a punch. She heard her dad's intake of breath as if it were him she'd struck. "And why isn't she the one on the phone with me, instead of electing you to do her dirty work? I thought my mother had more guts and honesty than that. But evidently there are lots of things I don't know about the woman who raised me."

"Hold it right there, young lady." Laney's dad broke in. "I insisted on being the one to talk to you first. You have no idea the agonies she's worked through—she and I both."

Laney hugged her knees to her chest. "Why did you stay with her, Dad?"

"Because I love her unconditionally, and what happened was my fault."

"Your fault!" Her voice rose an octave. "You were innocent. You didn't—"

"No, you and Grace were innocent. We tried to protect you. We failed with Grace, but we wanted to spare you the knowledge of what the Lord and some Godly counselors helped your mom and me to work out between us. You weren't the only one to attend therapy after Grace died, you know."

Laney swallowed more angry words. If her dad could speak calmly, she could, too. Maybe. "I still have no idea what makes you responsible for her infidelity."

"As our stories came out in the counseling sessions, I could finally see my sin of neglect. The affair began only a few months before Grace disappeared, but I divorced Loretta emotionally long before she strayed. My bad choices of how to spend my time and energy left her adrift. Alone."

"That doesn't excuse what she did." Laney's jaw clenched and her teeth ground together.

"No, it doesn't, but nothing excuses my sin,

either…except the blood of Jesus. Without that, we're all lost."

Words dried up on Laney's tongue. There was no argument against that statement. "I suppose you expect me to forgive Mom just like that." She snapped her fingers. "And everything will be hunky-dory."

"No, sweetie pie." His voice ached in Laney's ears. "Your mother and I know that nothing will be the same again." The words came out solemn, but not sad. "When life throws us curve balls, things never are, but one day they can be better than before—like your mom and me. Our marriage has never been stronger, and it keeps getting more like heaven on earth."

Laney frowned at her bare toes fisting against the sheets. "I'm happy for you and Mom. I am. But right now I…" Her voice trailed away.

"We understand. Your mom is on pins and needles to talk to you about this. She's okay with you yelling at her, but I'm not." He gave a wry chuckle. "So we'll give you some space to process, and then you two can visit woman to woman when you're ready."

Laney inhaled a long breath. "I'm not sure when that will be."

"We know that, too."

They ended the call, and Laney stared at the cradled phone. How did one regain shattered trust? She rubbed her eyes with the heels of her palms.

What if Noah's suspicion proved true, and Grace's death was connected to the adulterous affair? How would her mother live with herself then? If there was one thing Laney understood, it was the crushing burden of guilt.

Noah waited until nearly 9:00 a.m. to call Laney, though he'd been up for a couple of hours researching on the Internet for Adelle Addison. He might as well have stayed in bed for all the progress he made.

Faintly through the wall he could hear the phone ringing. She didn't answer. His stomach clenched. Did she leave her room alone? Had something happened to her?

He strode outside and pounded on her door. No response. He tried again as panic squeezed his vitals.

"Laney!" If anyone was still sleeping in the complex, they weren't anymore.

A rattling sound came from inside, and the door eased open to expose a bleary-eyed face, complexion pasty from sleep. Noah went weak at the knees. She was all right.

"What?" Laney blinked at him.

"You didn't answer your phone."

She ran splayed fingers through tousled hair. "I didn't hear it. I must have been lost in la-la land. After my dad called at five-thirty, I laid back down and—"

"You talked to your father? Did you discuss… last night?" He cringed at the pain that pinched her features. "What did he say?"

Her shoulders sagged. "He's known for years."

A spark of hope brightened Noah's insides. Maybe she'd see by that example that her relationship with her mother could heal, too. "So they worked out their marriage after all."

"So he says."

"Laney, I saw for myself that they have a strong relationship."

"I don't get it." She crossed her arms. "The affair tore the Addisons apart, and here my folks are better than ever."

"Tell you what," Noah said. "I'll let you grab a shower, then we can talk about what's next over breakfast. There's something I need your help with…or maybe one of your parents will have the answer."

Laney's face darkened. "You'll have to call them yourself, then. I'm not ready to speak to either of them right now. But let me talk to Bree when you make the call." She shut the door in his face.

Noah's heart ached to see her so devastated. She'd likely try to close everyone out while she nursed her pain. He knew that instinct well. Unfortunately, there was no time for processing and recovery right now.

Urgency rode him hard. They hadn't heard or seen any sign of Laney's tormenter here in Grand

Valley. Where was he—or she—and what was the monster planning next?

Forty-five minutes later, Noah sat across from Laney at the Pantry Café. She sipped sullenly at a cup of coffee.

Noah ran a finger up and down the handle of his cup. "If Adelle is part of this vendetta against your family, then she has a male accomplice."

"Obviously." Laney fidgeted with her silverware, gaze dull and distant.

Noah cautioned himself to patience. "The accomplice could be a boyfriend or a new husband, but in order to know, we need to find Adelle."

Her brows lifted. "And how do you propose to do that?"

Noah looked away and gave his own coffee some attention. *Lord, give me wisdom how to break through this bitter wall she's erected.* The prayer surprised him. He was doing that more and more. Softening his heart toward Laney was also softening his heart toward God. If only she didn't harden her heart toward relationships, because of her disappointment with her mother.

As he took a sip of his coffee, soft fingertips brushed the back of his free hand. "I'm sorry." Her gaze confirmed the apology. "Life is looking pretty sour to me right now. But that's not helpful, is it? I've still got to think about Bree." She said the words as if her daughter was the only family she had left. "What do you want to know?"

Noah set his cup down and let the waitress give him a refill. When she left, he leaned toward Laney.

"I'm coming up empty on finding the right Adelle Addison. There are dozens on Facebook, but only a few that might be the right age. I need you to take a look at their profile pictures."

She nodded. "I can do that."

"I've also run several public record searches, and there are Adelle Addisons all over the country, and a few in Minnesota, but none living in the vicinity of Cottonwood Grove."

Their breakfasts arrived, and conversation paused until the waitress withdrew.

Laney spread a napkin on her lap. "Would Adelle need to live near us? Maybe she looked me up the same way you're using to find her."

Noah poured syrup on his pancakes. "Maybe. But why wait eighteen years to do that and suddenly reappear? This has the feel of a vendetta that's been reawakened in response to a stimulus. You turning up in her neck of the woods would qualify. As a new teacher, your picture would have been in the area newspaper. She wouldn't even have had to encounter you face-to-face to know you're around."

Laney wagged her fork at him. "That's assuming she's the person we're looking for."

Noah nodded. "We only have suspicions and possibilities, but we need to locate her in order to eliminate or confirm her as a suspect."

Laney popped a bite of eggs into her mouth and chewed as if she were also chewing on her thoughts. "What if she's reverted to her maiden name?"

"Smart woman." Noah laughed. "I'm impressed. Her maiden name is what I needed to find out from your parents, if they know. I was pretty sure you wouldn't since you were only ten years old the last time you saw the Addisons."

A faint smile registered on Laney's face. "You're correct in assuming that the neighbor lady's maiden name was outside my scope of interest at that point in my life. But I meant what I said about you doing the calling."

"I can live with that." He didn't add "for now." Laney needed to make peace with her parents in her own time and her own way—after they caught the pervert trying to wreck her life. Until then, their barely budded relationship needed to stay on hold, too.

An hour later found him seated across from Laney in the motel office on his cell phone with Laney's dad. His laptop computer lay on top of the coffee table between them. The Facebook pictures had turned out to be a bust, and it looked as if the inquiry about Adelle was going to result the same.

"I have no idea what her maiden name was," Roland said. "How's my little girl holding up?"

Noah's heart throbbed. Daughters never outgrew being their daddy's little girl, and this daddy was hurting for his child. "Shell-shocked," Noah answered. "She's sitting here scowling because I'm talking about her. But she's a strong woman. Give her space, and she'll rise above the circumstances with the grace that she's always shown."

Laney blinked rapidly and turned her head away.

"Her mother and I are counting on that resilient spirit," Roland affirmed. "I'll let you talk to Loretta. She may know the answer to your question. Women chat about that sort of thing."

Seconds of muffled conversation passed on the other end, then Laney's mother came on the line. Her greeting was husky, as if tears had taken a toll on her voice.

"Roland says you'd like to know Adelle's maiden name. You can't really believe she could have had anything to do with Grace's disappearance."

Noah sought for the right words. This woman's pain was as great as Laney's, and it would grow a thousand times worse if it turned out that her affair spurred someone to hurt not only Grace, but Laney, as well.

"I haven't reached any conclusion yet," he told Loretta. "But this is an angle we must explore."

A harsh exhale came from the woman on the other end. "I suppose that's true. I'm going to have to disappoint you though. To my recollection, Adelle never told me her maiden na—oh, wait! She did mention that she graduated from high school in Ames, Iowa, if that's any help." She told him the year Adelle graduated.

"Cases have been cracked on less." Noah smiled. "Thank you. And one other thing. Your family is going to get through this. I've seen too much love between you to doubt that for a minute." Laney's gaze was hot on him, but not with anger. Unless he missed his guess, he was seeing a fierce resurgence of hope—a very good sign. "If Adelle turns out to be a party to the crimes against your family," he continued to Loretta, "remember that her evil actions were her own choice. Nothing you've done justifies hurting innocents."

A sob answered him. "Isn't that what the phone caller said? Players pay when innocents suffer? If that was Adelle's goal, then she's succeeded. Please stop her before she hurts another innocent. Please!"

"I'll do everything in my power. You can count on that." Noah's fingers dug into the chair upholstery. May God make him able.

"Good. We'll be praying."

"Thank you. I'll take all the divine assistance I can get." He nodded. "Now Laney would like to talk to Briana."

Loretta exhaled a soft sigh. "I understand. I'll get her."

While Laney chattered with false brightness to her daughter, Noah clicked on the computer to Web pages on Ames, Iowa, schools. Researching the alma mater was a long shot to find Adelle Addison's current name and address, but right now he'd take any shot at all.

While she talked to her daughter, Laney watched Noah search for answers. Jaw set, lips pressed together, cold gaze intent on the computer screen, this was Franklin Ryder, hunter of men, not Noah, the warm, strong school principal she'd known. Did she like what she saw? A tremor wafted through her. She didn't blame kidnappers for fearing this man.

Right now, there was no one she'd rather have on her side. But was he husband and father material? She didn't want to consider a Jekyl/Hyde personality for those positions. Her mother had stepped outside the bonds of marriage and done the unthinkable. Everything she thought she knew about the woman was now in question. How could she possibly consider trusting her heart—and her daughter's—to a man she knew less well than a parent she'd considered next to perfect?

"What was that, sweetie?" Lost in her turmoil she'd missed something Briana said.

Her daughter made an aggravated noise. "When you come to get me, I want Mr. Ryder to come, too. Promise?"

"Oh, honey." Laney sighed. "I don't know if that's going to be possible." Maybe she should have encouraged Pierce Mayfield's attention and let her daughter get to know him instead of attach to Noah. Pierce was a safe sort of person with a safe occupation—and no second career as a human bloodhound. She ignored the little voice that said the city bus driver was also boring and predictable. "Won't you be happy just to see me?" she said to Briana.

"I'll be happy to see you, Mama, but I'm going to wake up and see Mr. Ryder, too." Utter confidence flowed from the little voice.

"Wake up?" Laney chuckled. "Do you mean like Sleeping Beauty?"

"'Xactly," Briana affirmed.

Laney shared a giggle with her daughter. As dark as circumstances got, Briana could always brighten her day. But Laney would have to disappoint her little princess. After this investigation was over, it was probably best if Noah and she went their separate ways. Memory of that glorious kiss in the meadow nudged her, but she shoved the thought away. A solid relationship had to depend on more than a pulse-pounding moment. She'd learned that big-time with Clayton.

"Jackpot!"

Laney jerked at Noah's outburst. Triumph glowed from his face.

"I'll have to let you go now, sweetie," she told her daughter. She lowered the phone from her ear, pulse jumping. "What is it?"

He turned the computer screen her direction.

"The Ames High School Web site is complete with alumni association pages. Apparently, a reunion is pending for those who graduated the year Adelle did. See here?" He pointed to a short list of names. "These are the people the committee is still trying to locate. There's only one Adelle on the list."

Laney leaned forward and peered closely. "Adelle Birkstrom?" She straightened. "Okay. Maybe that's her maiden name, but if her old classmates can't find her, what makes you think you can?"

Noah smirked at her. "They may have her name, but they don't have a locality to search."

"And we do?"

He rose from his chair and sat down beside her on the couch so they could both see the computer screen. "I'm sticking to my theory that she lives near Cottonwood Grove. If I don't find an Adelle Birkstrom living in that area, then I could be all wet, or maybe she's remarried—in which case we're back to square one. But if I'm right…" His words trailed off as he brought up a map of west central Minnesota. "She probably doesn't live right in Cottonwood Grove, or you might have encountered her."

Laney nodded. "I think I would have recognized her."

He clicked open a fresh tab and went to the white pages directory. Tedious minutes passed as Noah entered various towns in connection with the name Adelle Birkstrom without success. Laney suppressed a yawn. She'd gotten little sleep last night and even less genuine rest.

Suddenly a result popped onto the screen.

Laney's brows climbed toward her bangs. "Adelle Birkstrom lives in Wellesly? That's only twelve miles from Cottonwood Grove."

Noah shook his head. "She doesn't necessarily live there, but she works there." He pointed to the column that said Helpful Info. The address given was listed as Job: followed by a business name. "This particular Adelle Birkstrom works at the Buffalo Bar and Grill."

Laney's eyes widened. "I've heard of the Buffalo, but nothing good. It's a dive." She pointed to the information. "Why wouldn't her home address come up?"

"Either she doesn't live in the town where she works, or she operates off a cell phone for personal calls. Only directory-available locations are listed in the white pages."

Rubbing her hands together, Laney watched Noah exhaust a search in every town within a sixty mile radius of Cottonwood Grove with no further results. "What now?"

He met her gaze. "Looks like we're going to see the Buffalo."

Laney's breath snagged in her throat. If Adelle Birkstrom was really Adelle Addison, would Laney soon stand face-to-face with her sister's murderer?

SIXTEEN

They were on the road in an hour. Overcast skies reflected the mood in the car. Noah glanced at his passenger out of the corner of his eye. Laney sat silent, studying her hands in her lap. She'd retreated to some place deep within herself.

Is this what she'd been like after Grace was taken? He understood the protective wall, but that moment in the meadow had encouraged him to believe he was becoming one of the people she'd count safe enough to include within, not shut out. Would he ever be that person, or had he built a sandcastle on a kiss?

Noah focused on the straight ribbon of asphalt weaving between a landscape of rolling fields, green with young growth of corn and soybeans. He needed to keep his head on straight. They were still eyeball-deep in a critical investigation. Now wasn't the time to explore a relationship. If only his heart understood what his head knew.

Laney shifted position. "Shall I try calling Sheriff Lindoll again?"

Noah shook his head. He'd like to shake that facade of cool professionalism right off her. "He'll get back to us when he can."

Noah had called the sheriff's office before leaving Grand Valley, but Hank was out on an emergency call. The dispatcher said as soon as he got back in she'd give him the message to call Noah.

Laney shifted in her seat. "Should we have notified the FBI about Adelle Addison?

"My police contact is Hank. He can tell Burns anything he considers relevant. We may be on a wild-goose chase, but it can't hurt to look in on things at home."

"And while we're at it, see for ourselves the water damage at the school." She nodded. "Maybe we can help Miss Aggie set things to rights."

The concern in her tone lifted Noah's spirits. That was the Laney he knew—thoughtful and giving. It was a good sign that she could think about something other than her own problems. "We'll do that." He smiled at her. "Why don't you try to rest while I drive?"

She shook her head. "Sleep isn't going to come right now. I'm too tense." She rubbed the back of her neck. "I can't figure out why the FBI didn't pick up on the possible motive in the Addison family."

Noah slowed the vehicle to pass through a small town. "You have to remember that everything looked fine with the Addisons during the investigation of Grace's death. George and Adelle didn't split up until after the investigation had gone cold."

She wrinkled her nose. "What about when they canvassed the neighborhood again after the backpack was found? They would have found George a wreck just like we did."

Noah wagged a finger at her. "But they didn't have you along to wring a gut reaction from him. A marriage breaking up, a son dying and one spouse going to seed isn't such a startling development over the years. I doubt Burns, or whoever he assigned to the canvas, thought to ask him if your family had anything to do with his problems, and I don't think good old George would volunteer that information."

Laney snorted. "So my presence brought out the worst in him?"

"It brought out the truth." Noah's cell phone played a tune, and he pulled it from his belt holder. "Ryder here."

"Sorry I didn't get back to you sooner," Hank said. "It's been one of those days when everything that can go wrong does." He huffed. "Say, you'll never guess what I found out today. Something did go right, after all." He chuckled.

"You tell me," Noah answered. "Then I'll hand you what I hope is a good break to balance the scales on your bad day."

"Sounds intriguing." The man's desk chair

squeaked. "I got a tip from a barfly over in Wellesly. Turns out Glen Crocker *does* have something going on the side."

"Let me guess the name of that something." Tingles ran up and down Noah's spine. "Adelle Birkstrom."

A beat of silence followed. "How did you steal my thunder?"

"Educated guess based on information Laney and I discovered in Grand Valley." He sent her a nod. She sat gnawing her bottom lip while he outlined their activities in Laney's old hometown.

Hank let out a low whistle. "Sorry to have to break it to you, but you don't have to show up for happy hour at the Buffalo. Adelle's got a house on the edge of Wellesly. Here, let me give you the address." He rattled off the information.

"We're about an hour away. We'll meet you there."

"Looking forward to it. Tell Laney good work."

"Will do. She can use all the encouragement she can get."

Noah closed the call and sent Laney a glance. "I'll give you one guess who Adelle Birkstrom's boyfriend is."

"Glen Crocker?" Her brows flew up.

"Bingo!"

She smiled. "Finally, the picture is beginning to take a form that makes sense. Glen must be her accomplice—the man who gave Mattie the doll and who hit me from behind. I wonder what's going on with the guy's foot?" Her nose wrinkled. "I guess that's a puzzle piece we'll have to look for later." She waved a hand. "Now all we have to do is catch them." Hope lit her gaze. "It would be so good to know my daughter and I are safe from these crazy people."

Noah bit back the question on the tip of his tongue. *Does that mean we're going to have a chance to make a family together?* The depth of his yearning for that opportunity haunted him.

"Hey, what?" His head swiveled to watch the FBI sedan that had been following them whip ahead. He chuckled. "Guess the feds got the word about something brewing."

Noah continued driving at a civilian pace. At last they turned onto a small road on the outskirts of the town of Wellesly, population five hundred and six.

"Whoa!" Noah stared ahead.

Laney sat wordless with her jaw slack.

A sheriff's SUV, a police cruiser and an ambulance sat in front of a house with their bubbles wheeling. An unmarked sedan also blocked the road—their FBI tail car. Bright crime scene tape ringed the house. Curious neighbors stood out on their lawns, gawking.

Noah parked up the block, and they got out.

"What do you suppose they found?" Laney murmured as they approached the area.

Her hand touched his, and Noah gladly wrapped his fingers around it.

A familiar figure broke away from a knot of law enforcement types near the house.

Hank strode toward them, face grim. "The bad day just went into the basement...literally."

"What's happened?" Noah asked.

Laney sidled closer to him, and he squeezed her hand.

Hank hooked a thumb in his belt. "Found Crocker's body in a basement storeroom. And the medical examiner says that from the level of decomp he's been dead for ten days to two weeks. Probably since the day he disappeared."

Noah hissed in a breath. "So he died *before* that backpack was left on the playground?"

Hank nodded. "Before or about that same time. Adelle Birkstrom is into this up to her eyeballs, but we still don't know who her accomplice is."

Laney's hand went slack in Noah's. Her breathing turned deep, fast and erratic. Alarmed, Noah wheeled toward her as she folded downward.

The nightmare wasn't over yet. It wasn't. Laney was still deep inside its black heart. No way out. Evil danced a step ahead of justice. Darkness curtained her vision. She groped for oxygen as her limbs gave way. Strong, warm arms came around her, preventing complete collapse, but she went stiff against them.

Somebody—the sheriff?—hollered for EMTs. Moments...or was it minutes?...later a mask closed over her nose and mouth, and soothing words from a familiar voice—a welcome voice—urged her to take deep breaths. Gradually, her lungs filled and her vision cleared. She found herself lying in the road, staring up at a man in a medical uniform. Noah's drawn features hovered just beyond.

Laney pushed the oxygen mask away. "I—I'm sorry. It was a panic attack. I used to get them, but I thought I had them licked…until all this started happening."

"It's all right, honey." Noah's gentle tones soothed.

"Perfectly understandable." The sheriff har-rumphed.

Laney made a move to rise, but the EMT's hand remained firm on her shoulder. "You should let us check your vitals."

Laney glanced up at Noah, who nodded. "O-okay. But not in the middle of the street."

Noah and the EMT helped her to a seat on the rear bumper of the ambulance. While the medical technician took her blood pressure and checked her heart and lungs, she stared into the gaping maw of Adelle Birkstrom/Addison's front door. Any second now a gurney would emerge, bearing another victim of this woman's twisted vengeance. Bile stung the back of her throat. Laney didn't want to be here when that happened.

Her gaze found Noah's. "Take me home."

"Home?"

"My apartment in Cottonwood Grove. I want to be surrounded by my familiar things right now."

The EMT nodded. "She checks out good to go."

With an arm around her shoulder, Noah guided her back to his car. She leaned into his warmth as tiny shivers wracked her insides. On the drive to Cottonwood Grove, Laney hugged herself, and searched for a smidgeon of comfort in the knowledge that at least they'd uncovered one guilty party in this ongoing tragedy, and they had a clear motive for what was going on. These nuggets were so much more than they'd had even yesterday, and yet so much worse than anything Laney ever dreamed possible.

"We're going to get through this," Noah said.

She managed a nod.

"Hank says Adelle has quite a china doll collection in her house. So we know where your nasty little gift came from."

She blew a long breath through her nose. "Another bit of the picture moves into focus. But why did she kill Glen Crocker?" Laney glared at Noah. "If he wasn't her accomplice, what did he have to do with her sick scheme?"

Noah shrugged. "He saw something he shouldn't. Or she tried to involve him in her plans, and he refused."

Laney rubbed her forehead. "I want to curl up in my bed and sleep the clock around."

"That's probably a good idea. The FBI will have a watcher outside your apartment."

She gave him a sidelong look. "I don't suppose you're going to get some rest, too."

"Later, maybe." That bloodhound look was back on his face.

"Don't forget to check on the flood damage at the school."

"I plan to get around to that, too."

Laney stretched her legs in front of her. "Do me a favor and call my parents with an update."

Noah frowned, but nodded.

By about 9:00 p.m., they reached her apartment door. The confident stride and the warmth of his presence beckoned her to let him hold her, if only for a few moments. But that would encourage him needlessly. When this was over, if ever it was, she and Briana needed a fresh start elsewhere.

Laney unlocked her door, then turned toward him. His piercing green eyes searched her face for answers that had nothing to do with the case.

"Thank you for everything," she said simply, then entered her apartment and closed the door. She couldn't afford to acknowledge the disappointment on his face.

Alone in her apartment, even familiar things looked foreign. But then, her whole world had turned inside out. She really ought to call her mom and dad herself, and she missed Briana like an ache in her soul, but she couldn't bring herself to pick up the phone.

Her feet carried her into her bedroom. She

dropped her purse on the floor, stripped off her outer clothes and collapsed into the comfort of her sheets and coverlet.

The persistent singing of her cell phone brought her eyes open. How long had she slept? Light crept around the corners of the window shade, but was it evening or morning? The cell phone's nagging ceased. Who was trying to call her? Noah? She forced leaden limbs to carry her over to her purse. As she reached inside, the cell began to sing again. She pulled the instrument out and stared at the caller ID. She didn't recognize the number. Chills skittered around her insides.

She flipped the phone open. "Hello?"

"We've been driving through the night from Louisville, Kentucky," a cheerful female voice announced. Laney's heart seized. That voice hadn't changed much in eighteen years. "It won't be long until we're back where it all began," Adelle continued.

"Mrs. Addison?" Laney's voice quavered.

The woman chuckled. "Birkstrom, please. You and Mr. Ryder have put a few things together, I see. Where are you, little Laney? Are you alone? I hope so. We need to see you and resolve this matter. But only you. No police. No Ryder."

"Where are you and who's with you?" Laney's grip fisted around the phone.

"All will become clear soon." The eerily soothing tone raised goose bumps on Laney's skin. "Once again, where are you, Laney Thompson?"

"Cottonwood Grove." Her heart pounded. Had she made a mistake admitting her location? But it seemed the only way to move this conversation along and find out what Adelle was after.

"Too bad. We'd hoped you were still in Grand Valley. Then you wouldn't have so far to travel. If you leave now, you can meet us at the trysting place before the clock strikes twelve noon. Not a second later."

"Trysting place? Where?"

"You will be told what you need to know when you need to know it." Ice would have been warmer than this woman's voice. "Remember. No police. No nosy Ryder. No calls out, and no calls received during your drive time. When you arrive, we will check to see how you have used your cell phone. And be punctual, or the little princess pays the ultimate price." The airwaves went dead.

The little princess? They had Briana! How? When? It didn't matter.

Sweat oozing from her pores, Laney battled her galloping heart and heaving lungs into submission. She could *not* afford a panic attack. She *had* to save her daughter.

The clock said nearly 7:00 a.m. Adelle was right. Unless she raced out the door this very instant and risked arrest for speeding, she would never make the twelve noon deadline…that is, if she'd understood correctly that the trysting place was near Grand Valley. That's were this travesty "all began," wasn't it?

Laney threw clothes on. No FBI? No Noah? How could she face these monsters without his support? But she couldn't risk her daughter's life to gain a helping hand. And she sure couldn't risk law enforcement pressure—not after the horror story Noah had told her about his fiancée's death when Burns and his bunch got involved.

Snatching up her purse and car keys, she left the apartment at a run and didn't bother to lock up. *God, help me,* her heart cried. *Noah, please find me,* a piece of it echoed.

At the bottom of the stairs she peeked out the front window. The unmarked FBI sedan sat across the street. Fine. Let them watch all they wanted for someone to have a go at her. They wouldn't expect the woman they thought they were protecting to sneak out the locked rear service entrance and drive away.

Soon Laney was on the road out of town at the wheel of her compact car. Her whole body trembled. She'd have to stop for gas at some point and chew up precious minutes she didn't have to spare. How could she possibly reach this unknown rendezvous on time?

And if she didn't meet the deadline, would she arrive to find her daughter's body? Or worse, no body, only pools of telltale lifeblood, screaming her failure as a mother. Just like she failed as a sister.

SEVENTEEN

At 7:45 a.m., Noah padded to his kitchen, yawning. He'd awakened later than he intended, but then he'd been burning the candle at both ends for days now. Hopefully, Laney had gotten some rest last night, too. If only he'd had the right to stay with her in her apartment. Thoughts of her alone and processing another death in this bizarre case had disturbed his slumber.

Despite the tragic development of Glen Crocker, he hoped they were closing in on Adelle and her mystery accomplice. There could well be something in her house that would give them a clue to her whereabouts and even the accomplice's identity. After checking out progress in repairs to the school building last evening, he'd returned to the crime scene in Wellesly to discover Agent Burns had arrived full of "spit and vinegar" as his grandmother used to say. The agent hadn't been too delighted to see Noah, but the feeling was mutual.

He'd returned home around ten and hit the sack. A phone call to Hank this morning should get him up to speed on developments, and he'd decide from that information what rock to turn over next in the hunt for a couple of very sick perps. The sooner this case wrapped up, the sooner he could concentrate on being the kind of man Laney needed to round out her family.

Smiling, he dumped coffee grounds into a filter and turned the machine on. Funny how he'd resisted the thought of romance with a coworker. The school district didn't have any policy against it. In fact, he knew teachers and fellow administrators in other districts who were married to each other. Now that the smart, gentle, courageous woman had melted through his defenses, the reasons he'd given himself for remaining aloof sounded more like self-serving excuses to protect a wounded heart. He'd do whatever it took to be with her.

His cell sounded as he poured cereal into a bowl. He checked the caller ID. Hank. "What's up?"

"Not much, I'm afraid. This Adelle woman is a queen bee schemer. The feds aren't happy at how little she left behind for them to go on. We do know from the neighbors that her pickup truck gone, and a little pop-up camper she kept in the backyard. We've got an APB out on those vehicles, but that's about it since last night."

"That's all you can do, then." He did hate the waiting part of this game.

They ended the call. Noah poured milk onto his cereal as he thumbed Laney's apartment number into the phone. It rang and rang, then went to voice mail. He frowned. Was she sleeping that soundly? He tried her cell, but that went to voice mail, too. Abandoning the coffee in the auto-shutoff machine and his milk and cereal on the counter, Noah trotted from his apartment.

He was an idiot for not bunking on a sleeping bag in her hallway. What a fool to think an FBI watcher outside would be enough. If she'd simply made a trip to the store and left her cell in her apartment, he'd wring her neck. But his gut said something was wrong.

Laney flexed her fingers around the steering wheel of her car. It had nearly killed her not to answer Noah's call, but she didn't dare leave evidence on her cell that she'd spoken to someone. If only she could give him some type of clue where she was headed. She'd been in such a panic when she left her apartment that taking a few seconds to leave him a note had been beyond her mental processes. What was she thinking to confront these ruthless people by herself? But now she was on the road, and she couldn't take time to stop.

Her cell played again, and she checked the window. It was her parents. Were they only now discovering that Briana was missing? It would be nearly 9:00 a.m. in Louisville, but Bree sometimes slept that late when no one got her out of bed. Then again, Laney gnawed her lower lip, she only had Adelle Addison's word that Briana was at their mercy. Nothing someone like her said could be trusted.

Laney's phone beeped that she had a message. Should she check it? Adelle hadn't told her she couldn't access her voice mail. Listening to a message shouldn't qualify as communicating with anyone. She punched in her voice mail access code and put the cell to her ear. *C'mon, Dad...or Mom even...tell me the Bree-Bee is all right.* Then she'd turn this car around and—

"Laney!" Panic saturating her dad's voice confirmed the worst. A sob left her throat. "Where are you? Oh, dear God, help us! We went in to wake Briana up, and she's not there! Just a life-size china doll in her bed. Call us. Now!" Dad's harsh breathing mingled with the faint sound of her mother weeping in the background. "We've called the authorities, and we're going to call Noah next. We think Briana was taken by the private security guard on duty last night. He's missing, too. Oh, my Laney-girl, I'm so sorry." Dad's voice broke, and the message cut off.

Waves of ice water washed over Laney. She put the phone down and returned both hands to the wheel. Her jaw clenched. Adelle Addison might think that her plot to destroy the Thompson family was poised to succeed. She'd reckoned without the wrath of a mother. Heaven help the woman when Laney caught up with her.

A furious moan escaped her lips. If she had to stop at a convenience store for gas, she'd better take the opportunity to arm herself with something…anything. But what?

As he dashed into Laney's apartment building, Noah waved at the FBI agent in the car across the street, but didn't wait to see if the guy got out. Noah took the stairs two at a time to the third floor. Sweating from nerves, rather than exertion, he hammered his fist against her apartment door. The latch let out a *snick* and gave way. Her door gaped open several inches. Noah stared in horror, then charged through calling her name. If an intruder was inside there was no point in being subtle now.

The ticking of a wall clock and the hum of the refrigerator answered him. He raced up the hall. The first bedroom featured a neatly made twin bed and pink princess decorations. He trotted into the next room, obviously Laney's, with its cheerful but conservative furnishings. Clothing strewed the floor and covers were flung nearly off the bed— evidence of haste in the neat room.

"What's going on, Ryder?" The agent's voice called him back to the living room. The man stood with his hand inside his jacket where the bulk of a handgun showed.

"She's gone," Noah told him. "Left in a hurry.

On her own or coerced, I don't know. We need to see if her car is in the garage."

On the way down the stairs, the agent trailed, talking urgently on his phone. They reached the garage. Laney's stall was empty. Had she driven away on her own power or with someone who had her under duress?

Noah's cell phone sang out. "Ryder, here."

"She's gone," a gravelly male voice grated in his ear.

Who was it? The accomplice? The voice was vaguely familiar, but…altered. "Yes, we know. Who's calling?"

"I-it's me. Roland Thompson."

"Roland?" No wonder the voice sounded familiar, but the man had either been crying or yelling himself hoarse. "How do you know Laney's missing?"

"Laney? No, I mean Briana."

Noah's knees went weak. He reached out and supported himself with an arm against the garage wall. "Briana's gone, too?" His mind raced. Of course! That was the only button those kidnapping creeps could push that would guarantee Laney would do anything they said—including take off for parts unknown without telling a soul. "When did Briana go missing?"

The FBI agent lowered his phone from the side of his head and stared at him.

"Sometime in the night. We think it was the

hired security guard. He's gone, too. Only he wasn't the right one."

"What do you mean?" Noah's brows drew together.

Roland hissed in a long breath. "Another dead body. Maybe. The security company just confirmed that our guy wasn't the one scheduled for last night. FBI agents are on their way to the real security guard's house, and some are on the way here."

Noah went still on the inside. "What did the imposter look like?"

"About mid-thirties, and he was bald with scars on his head. Looked like a real tough guy. As a security guard, his appearance was comforting. Hah!"

Disappointment ate at Noah's insides. That description fit no one familiar. The mystery accomplice's identity remained a mystery. "If our perps, or at least one of them, were in Louisville last night, then they must have set up a meeting place with Laney."

"I can't believe she's gone, too." Roland's statement came out edged with hysteria.

Next to him, the agent's phone rang, and the guy wandered away to take the call. He'd no doubt be getting the same information as Noah was hearing right now…and maybe more, if the feds had a line on the identity of the fake security guard.

Laney's father let out a whimper. "Find our babies, will you, please?"

The other man's ragged plea twisted Noah's heart. "I'll do my best."

He turned around to see the FBI agent striding away. "...put an APB out on her car," Noah heard him saying, but the guy didn't afford him a backward glance. So much for information-sharing between the P.I. and the FBI. As if that was going to happen!

"Let me in on any further developments," he said to Roland, and they ended the call.

Noah gripped his closed phone. Find Laney and Briana? Yes, that was top priority. But unless the cops got lucky and spotted her car, where did he start looking?

Laney gnawed her lower lip. She was driving her own car. Surely, law enforcement would have an APB out on it. She hadn't seen any patrol cars, but it was only a matter of time before she passed one. Would the cops follow her to her meeting with the kidnappers? Could that cost her daughter's life? Or worse, what if the police stopped her on the road? What had the woman been thinking! Adelle's plan couldn't work.

Her poor little Briana. How scared she must be. Laney's chest ached. Anguish, and anger, and fear balled into a tight knot under her breastbone.

Her phone played. The ID was the same number that had been Adelle's earlier. Sucking in a deep breath, she answered.

"Have you been a good girl?" the woman demanded.

"No cops. No Noah. No phone calls. Oh, er, I did listen to voice mail. So, yes, I've done everything you asked of me. Now I want to talk to my daughter."

"I'm afraid that's not possible."

Laney stiffened. "She's okay. She's not—"

"Relax, Mama. She's sleeping. I doubt she even knew we removed her from her bed."

Drugged, then? But she didn't ask that question aloud. "Who's we?"

"In good time, dear. By now, you are the subject of a manhunt, as are we. I need you to stop at a friend's house along the route."

"Stop! I won't make the rendezvous on time if I—"

"Relax. The stop will take less time than filling a tank of gas." Adelle gave directions to a farm place near Laney's current location and instructions about what she was to do when she got there.

Laney prayed she could remember the details in her rattled condition. Fortunately, it was a simple turn-off and then one more turn. She pulled onto a rutted driveway through an overgrown grove. Moments later, she burst into the clear in front of a dilapidated clapboard house. Bleary windows in the two-story structure looked out on a weedy lawn dotted with vehicles in various stages of disrepair. A pudgy man in a dirt-streaked muscle shirt and grease-spotted jeans ambled off the porch as she stopped her car.

Laney eased out of the driver's seat, eyeing the seedy-looking character who approached with a set of car keys extended in her general direction. But his gaze wasn't on her. His wide eyes were locked on her car. She'd bought it new when she got the teaching job in Cottonwood Grove a year ago.

"You get that one." He jerked a thumb toward a rust-bucket of a low-slung coupe. "Don't look pretty, but she runs okay. You'll get there anyway."

Laney snatched the keys. "Don't you care that Adelle has taken my daughter and is going to kill her if I don't reach a certain place on time?"

The man tucked in his blubbery chin, making him look rather like a toad. "Don't know nothin' about such nonsense, but I'd do about anything for Adelle. Sounds like you'd best be rollin' out of here, Missy."

Laney opened her mouth, but pressing her case would get nowhere with this man. He was rubbing his hands along the smooth paint on the hood of her car. Adelle must have promised him the vehicle, which said loud and clear what plans she had for Laney when they met. Laney hopped into the coupe and wrinkled her nose. It smelled like the inside of a dirty sock. Her gaze narrowed as she put the old clunker into gear. They'd just see who came out on top in a fight for Briana.

Back out on the highway, she checked the gas

gauge. Full, of course. Now she'd have no need to stop again and no opportunity to pick up some sort of a weapon. Even a pocketknife would have been welcome. The vehicle switch also meant no possibility of the police spotting her. She had clear sailing to Grand Valley.

But she was also quite alone. Even Noah couldn't find her now.

God, if ever You've heard my prayers, please, hear me now. Help!

Noah sat in his darkened school office with his eyes closed and prayed for God to guide his thoughts. All he knew to do now was what had worked for him in the past when he reached an apparent dead end in pursuit of an elusive abductor. Now that one of the kidnappers was known—the probable brains of the operation—he could put himself in her place, follow her thought processes, explore options from her point of view, and hopefully arrive where she was. When he was a rookie cop, fellow officers had scoffed at his untrained attempts to "profile" suspects and figure out their next move…until he kept being right. If ever he needed that innate ability to hit a bull's-eye, it was now.

This was how he'd tracked Renee and her abductor to the wilds of Northern Minnesota, when the FBI with their trained profilers had been two steps behind him. He'd found them, all right, but the ending hadn't been good. This time *couldn't* end like last time. He shoved his fears into oblivion and gave himself over to Adelle—her needs, her drives, her goals.

He was Adelle Addison, consumed by hatred and a deep, pulsing need for revenge. She was cruel and clever and had no compunction about tormenting the innocent. In fact, she used them as tools to punish those she viewed as unforgivable. She lashed out at Loretta Thompson by killing the most vulnerable daughter. Now she wanted to finish the job by taking the rest of Loretta's offspring from her. She punished her husband, George, by taking away his only son.

Noah gasped and sat up. Maybe the way Watts died wasn't the way she told George. Did Adelle murder her own son to wreak her vengeance? He needed to find out more of the circumstances surrounding that death. How that might lead to her current whereabouts—and Laney's—he wasn't sure, but it was an unexplored avenue.

And there was another vital, but unanswered question about the affair that set off this tragic chain of events—where in that little burg did George and Loretta find a place to tryst? Noah got on the phone to Loretta. It was a painful question that had to be asked.

Loretta cleared her throat several times after he requested the information. "We-e-ell, as you know, George ran a construction business. He had contracts all over the place, bigger communities. We'd preplan a hotel and meet there."

"Different places?"

"Yes, many."

Disappointment soured his stomach. "So there was no private hideaway."

Loretta gasped. "I'd forgotten," she said. "The very day Gracie went missing, George told me he'd bought a small property in the country, some place by a river, so we wouldn't have to use hotel rooms in the public eye anymore."

Hope resurrected. "Can you tell me how to get there?"

"No, I can't. We never used it. Grace went missing that afternoon." Laney's mother paused. "The tragedy sobered me up. It was like I'd been drunk and not thinking straight. I suddenly realized what I was doing and knew it had to stop."

"Thank you, Loretta. I know this was hard for you to talk about. I'll take it from here."

"I wish I could have been more help."

Noah wished it, too, but he reassured her and hung up. Then he got on the phone to the court-houses in counties surrounding Grand Valley. None of them had any record of George Addison owning property other than his house. The man must have sold his love nest after the Thompsons left town.

Noah sighed. Only one source remained for the location, and he was likely perched on a stool in Bucky's Bar.

Noah got on the phone with Hank. "I need a couple of things," he told the sheriff. "See what you can dig up on Watts Addison's death about fourteen years ago. Circumstances were reported to be a car accident. I'd do the research myself, but I need to be in the air."

"In the air!"

"That's the other favor." Noah tapped a pencil on his desk blotter. "Do you know any pilots around here who'd rent their plane and services to leave pronto from the municipal airfield? I need to get to Grand Valley—like yesterday."

Hank gave a low hum. "Yeah, I think I do. I'll set it up and have him meet you out there."

"Great!" Noah pulled the receiver away from his ear and headed it for the cradle.

"Wait!"

Noah returned the received to his ear. "What's up?"

"Just thought you might want to know the FBI are all over that town, including Burns himself, watching for Adelle."

"I suppose they're particularly focused on George Addison."

"You got it."

Noah frowned. That was who he needed to speak to, and without FBI knowledge. He'd have to finesse something when he got there. "Thanks. Anything else?"

"They found Adelle's pickup and pop-up abandoned in an RV park near Louisville."

"So she's not driving that rig anymore." Noah snorted. This woman was wicked clever. "Any word on Laney's vehicle?"

"Negative. But they did find the real security guard for the Thompson home shot and left for dead in his living room. He's in surgery, and they don't know if he'll make it."

A bitter taste filled Noah's mouth. Adelle and her accomplice made Bonnie and Clyde look like stand-up comics. *Laney, what got into you to head straight into their hands?* But he knew. A mother's love. Now if only his love could track them down.

She had to stop, even if it were just for five minutes. There was no way around it. She couldn't go into this confrontation with nothing to create an element of surprise so her daughter could get away. Besides, her bladder was about ready to burst.

In a town an hour from Grand Valley, she pulled up in front of a convenience store. Counting every precious second, Laney did her business and got back on the road—one new item in her purse and one tucked into her shoe.

Her phone played as she accelerated out of town. Adelle.

"You're alone?" the woman asked.

"Yes. How's Briana?" If only her voice didn't tremble when she spoke.

"The little princess still slumbers."

"Don't you harm a hair on her head, Adelle. I—"

"Save the threats. I will text you the directions to the trysting place." The woman closed the call.

Gut churning, Laney waited for the beep that would announce the arrival of the text message. Within a minute it came. She studied the directions. She would have never guessed the location. No one else would, either. As far as anyone knew, right next to the state forest like that, there was nothing but trees and wilderness for miles and miles. And yet the site was so very close to where the last evidence of Gracie was found.

Laney rested a hand on her purse and scrunched her toes in her shoe, feeling the solid presence. At least she was heading for the showdown armed… sort of.

Armed and terrified.

EIGHTEEN

Noah flew into the Rochester, Minnesota, airport and rented a car for the last short leg of the journey south. He was pulling into Grand Valley when his phone rang.

"Have you got something good for me, Hank?"

The sheriff snorted. "Just another puzzle. Listen up."

Noah's eyes widened as Hank talked. He'd been oh-so-right that Watts was a key to this case, but oh-so-wrong about how that key worked.

Ten minutes later, Noah waved a six-pack of Pepsi toward Bing, seated on his stool-throne in front of the body shop in Grand Valley.

The old man licked his lips, but kept his hands on his knees. "You say you need me to do what?"

"I need you to help me get a chance to talk to George Addison without attracting FBI attention."

Bing cackled. "That'll be some trick. The feds are thick as ticks around town. Old George, though, he's complainin' loud and long that they asked him a bunch of questions, but he wouldn't tell 'em nothin'. How do you think you're gonna have any luck with that mule in manskin?"

"But I think I might have some leverage for his tongue."

"So run that by me again what I gotta do?" Bing reached for the six-pack.

"I need you to go into Bucky's Bar and give George a message for me. Then come out and distract the FBI agent who will be following the guy. I need to make a clean getaway with Addison."

Bing's mouth moved as if he was chewing cud. "And you say a private chat with George might help Laney and her little girl?"

Noah nodded.

"Then you can count on me." The man hugged his six-pack.

Ten minutes later, Noah was parked up the block from Bucky's Bar in a grocery store lot. Soon George emerged from the bar, staring around as if he'd never seen sunlight before. The man made his unsteady way up the block toward the grocery store. Behind him, Bing wandered out of the bar, and then a younger man in a sports shirt and slacks—the FBI tail.

About halfway up the block, Bing whirled toward the young agent, pressing a hand against his chest. He grabbed the agent's shirt as he folded toward the ground. Unearthly wails carried faintly to Noah from the old gentleman. Noah winced. The gossip-fount of Grand Valley was an overactor.

Without a backward glance toward the commotion, George continued his bleary-eyed charge toward the parking lot where Noah waited. Bent over Bing and locked in the oldster's grip, the agent got on his radio. Bing's hysterics revved up another notch, then abruptly ceased as he went limp. The agent began checking vitals, feeling the neck, listening at the chest, as George half fell into the passenger seat of Noah's car.

Smooth as glass, Noah pulled out of the parking lot. He grinned and shook his head. Bing had missed his calling. The stage had lost a real ham.

"Whaddaya want?" His passenger demanded. "The old geezer shaid you had important information about my shun Watts."

"First of all," Noah shot the man a level look, "if there are any ashes in that urn Adelle sent you, they don't belong to Watts. Second, I need you to tell me how to get to that place you bought for you and Loretta the day Grace Thompson disappeared."

Gaze half on her watch and half on the rutted woodland road, Laney took the final turn toward the trysting place practically on two wheels. The second hand flipped past twelve noon as the ancient car barreled between endless forestation. Massive gnarled tree branches hung over the dirt track as if poised to reach out leafy arms and stop her. Laney raced on, missing them by inches.

Her breath came in gasps, and the blood roared in her ears. *Hang on, Bree, honey. Mama's coming for you.*

The vehicle burst free of the trees into a weed-grown clearing. Laney jammed on the brakes and skidded to a screeching stop in front of a dilapidated cabin with no glass in the windows and a porch that was falling away from the structure.

She had no time to reconnoiter or plan. Laney dove out of the car. "I'm here!"

The cry was swallowed by the dense woods. Her feet pounded the rotting boards of the porch, and she burst through the door of the cabin, lungs pumping. Then she stopped still and stared around.

A square table sat in the middle of a bare room with three ladder-backed chairs around it. Animal debris scattered on the floor and a rank smell testified to recent four-legged habitation. She didn't blame any wild creatures for running from the two-legged skunks who had set up this rendezvous.

Ahead, a doorway led into a second room. A soft scraping noise came from that direction. Chest tight, Laney backed away and came up against the edge of the front door frame.

A familiar figure stepped out from the inner room into a narrow stream of sunlight from the open front door. Not Adelle. Laney's voice dried up in her throat as she locked gazes with the last person she ever expected to see at this moment in time.

He motioned toward a chair with a hand that clutched a sturdy rope. "Have a seat, Laney."

Noah sped out of town as fast as he dared to avoid drawing attention. George Addison gave terse directions—turn here, go there. And in between he muttered terrible curses down on his sadistic wife.

The man seemed to have sobered up considerably as he absorbed the news that his son was alive. Noah could promise that much anyway. Hank had said that there was an accident report that noted grave injuries in a motor vehicle accident, as well as a newspaper obituary for Watts Addison, but evidently a person couldn't believe everything they read in the paper. However, there was no death certificate officially filed anywhere in the country. The certificate George had waved at the FBI must be as false as the urn of ashes.

Oh, yes, Noah now knew the true identity of Adelle's mystery accomplice. He just didn't know what identity the former Watts had taken after news of his death was so greatly exaggerated. And until they found out, George refused to leave the vehicle, even when Noah threatened to toss him out bodily. The man swore he'd tell the FBI where Noah had gone and have the feds out there before Noah had a chance to get Laney clear.

He caved at that prospect. It hadn't been in his plan to drag the drunken mess along, particularly when he had to put up with the guy's unwashed odor and liquor fumes. However, he understood the parental instinct.

Briana, hang on, little princess. I'm on my way and so is your mama.

For all he knew Laney could be at the site this moment, confronting terrors unspeakable. He pressed the gas harder.

Laney stood her ground. "Pierce! What are you doing here? Where's Briana?"

"We'll get to that." Adelle's voice came from behind her, and Laney whirled. The woman stood on the grass beyond the porch, aiming a pistol in her direction. "Obey my son."

"Your son?" Laney stumbled forward in a daze as Adelle followed her into the room. As she sank into the chair, Laney stared at the man she knew as Pierce Mayfield. He began to tie her wrists to the chair arms. "You don't look one bit like Watts." Her gaze darted to a smirking Adelle. "Did you have another child no one knew about?"

Grinning, Pierce straightened. He reached up and pulled the brown wig from his head, revealing a scarred, bald pate. "I had a terrible accident. My face was so smashed up, they had to reconstruct it over time and many surgeries. I asked them to make certain changes in my appearance as part of the process. The surgeons did an excellent job, don't you think?"

"Watts? Adelle?" Laney looked from one to the other.

Her former neighbor lady hadn't changed much in appearance. She was still a slender, almost rail-thin woman, with a sharp chin and a long neck. But she'd gained a few wrinkles around her hazel eyes, and Laney would bet money that the solid brown hair color came from a bottle.

"What have you done with my daughter?" Laney glared at her captors.

They glanced at each other and snickered.

She kicked at Watts, grazing his left shin, and he quick-stepped backward. Scowling like thunder, he cursed her. Adelle laughed. Laney stared at Watts's shoes. He wore the leather lace-ups she'd seen on him at the last day of school party, but now the seam near the left big toe was spreading and giving way.

"Your foot was hurt in the accident, too," Laney said. "How come you don't walk with a limp?"

"Years of practice." Watts lifted his chin.

Adelle sniffed. "And he spends a ton on replacing shoes to wear in public when the edge starts giving way."

Laney narrowed her gaze on Watts. "I hope your foot hurts like an abscessed tooth." She wiggled her wrists to test the binding. Very tight. Much good her feeble "weapons" did her now that she couldn't get to them. And besides, she mentally smacked herself, she'd left her purse in the car. "All I care about is my daughter. Where is she?"

Adelle sighed like a long-suffering teacher. "I told you the princess is sleeping."

Laney's heart squeezed in on itself. Did the woman mean Briana was really asleep or a more permanent kind of slumber? There was no clue to the truth in the evil glee etched on this woman's face.

"Keep an eye on her." Adelle nodded toward her son and went out the door.

Laney flexed her hands around the arm of the chair, desperate plans forming and failing in her head. "Watts, you can't really want to be part of this insane scheme. We were playmates. And Briana's done nothing to you."

She could scarcely fathom that she'd known this scarred and cold-eyed man as the kindly, but boring Pierce Mayfield and also as the fourteen-year-old daredevil boy whose voice had barely begun to change when the Thompsons left Grand Valley.

The familiar stranger sneered at her. "Mom stuck by me through everything. I do what she says and like it."

Adelle came back inside, carrying Laney's purse. She dumped the contents onto the table and sifted through them. One object she hefted with a laugh. "Bug spray? You came prepared for the Minnesota woods, all right." She set the can down and examined Laney's cell phone. "Looks like you were a good girl and restrained the urge to call for help."

"Forget this vendetta," Laney said. "Just tell me where my daughter is and get out of here. By now there are FBI agents crawling all over this area. They'll find this place eventually. It doesn't take a rocket scientist to figure out that you two might have returned to the scene of your original crime." Was Noah nearby, too? *Oh, please, God. Guide him.*

Adelle flipped the phone shut and tossed it onto the table. The woman eyed Laney dispassionately. "I assume you're referring to Grace. That was no crime. It was an—"

"Adelle!" The strident cry came from outside, and whipped all heads in that direction.

"Adelle Addison!" The bellow came again. "Where's my son?"

Noah froze at the edge of the woods on the west side of the moldering cabin. Blast that drunken fool! He'd ordered George to stay in the car he'd parked out of sight up the drive. Noah had seen the gun in Adelle's hand when she stepped outside and grabbed Laney's purse from that rattletrap out front, and he didn't need someone getting shot on his account. Too late now.

In front of the cabin, the soused father kept hollering. There was nothing Noah could do for the man. His efforts had to be for Laney. Noah looked down at the tire iron in his hand. Not much good against a bullet, but George might be the witless decoy he needed…if the guy didn't catch one of those bullets first.

Noah crept toward a glassless side window of the cabin.

"Time for you to die, George," Adelle yelled back.

"That's not part of the plan, Mom," a familiar voice protested.

Noah's neck hair stood on end. He mentally smacked himself. Watts, aka Pierce, had been under their noses the entire time, a slimy little worm ingratiating himself to the community and trying to romance the object of his hatred. Lower than sludge was an understatement.

"He's got to pay, too," Adelle hissed to her son.

"I can't let you kill my dad," Watts answered.

"He's a pig." Adelle's voice had risen to a screech. Good, she was getting worked up. Maybe she'd get careless. "Look at him," she went on. "The slob can hardly stand up."

Foosteps retreated toward the front door, followed by a second pair, heavier than the first. Were they both leaving the building? Better and better.

He wasn't going to get a clearer opportunity. Taking a deep breath, Noah heaved himself through the window.

* * *

Bickering, Adelle and Watts disappeared out the front door. Skin chaffing, Laney worked frantically at her bonds. She had seconds…maybe. A shot sounded outside, then a yelp. Laney jerked. Had the death toll just risen? Familiar hands began working at the ropes.

"Noah, you found me." Laney's heart leaped as she gazed into his tense face. His hair was a mess and sported a piece of green leaf and his face was scratched, but he'd never looked so handsome. How she loved this man!

"Are you all right?" His green gaze searched hers.

"I'm fine, but they won't say what they've done with Bree."

Adelle's gun barked again, followed by the tinkle of shattered glass. A car window most likely. Shouts and curses and running feet sounded.

"Don't waste time with those knots," Laney told Noah. "There's a pocketknife in my right shoe."

"Brilliant woman." Noah bent and came up with the instrument. He stared at the miniature object. "You call this a knife?"

"It was all the convenience store had."

He sawed at the ropes. One side parted.

"This thing is small but mighty," Noah pronounced.

The second side began to fray as hard breathing and creaking boards announced the return of her captors.

"Here." Noah pressed the knife into Laney's free hand. "Finish the job and dive out the window."

He snatched up a tire iron from the floor beside him and moved to meet the pair with the gun.

If he could just stall for time, Laney might get away. Noah took up a post beside the open door, prepared to clobber the first person who stepped inside. If he could knock the gun away, he might survive the encounter. If not, well, Laney stood a chance of losing her kidnappers in the dense trees.

A figure stepped inside, and Noah swung at his head. Watts staggered and went down, bleeding from the side of a bald pate. Adelle lunged through the door, firing. The wild shot spanged off the crowbar, wrenching it from Noah's grip.

He lunged for the woman, and they grappled for control of the gun. Her wiry strength challenged him, but he began to get the advantage. Then a leg swept his feet out from under him, and he whumped flat onto his back. Air whooshed from his lungs.

Watts cackled. "Gotcha!" The man struggled to his feet.

Noah stared, fighting to suck air back into his lungs. How could the guy get up so fast? The blow Noah had delivered should have KO'd an ox.

"Metal plate." Watts knocked on the side of his head.

As Noah finally heaved a breath of oxygen, the

black maw of Adelle's pistol appeared above his face. A click announced the weapon was cocked.

The woman glared down at him, lips drawn back from white teeth. "Bye-bye, P.I."

Breath sawing as hard as the knife, Laney cut the last strand of rope binding her wrist. She leaped up and snatched the can of bug spray. Scarcely sparing a nanosecond to aim, she hit the button in the direction of Adelle's face.

Screeching obscenities, the woman scuttled backward, one hand scrubbing at her eyes. The hand that clutched the gun waved crazily in the air. The weapon blasted, and a buzz like a speeding hornet swept past Laney's ear. She kept spraying toward Adelle, then toward a snarling Watts, who covered his eyes with his forearm and charged toward her. Laney dodged, and he swept past, caught himself and turned, shaking his head like a frustrated bull. Blood still trickled from the split skin on the side of his head.

On the edge of her vision, Laney watched Noah roll and stagger to his feet, coughing and shaking his head. The fallout from the spray must have caught him full in the face. Still swiping at her face and cursing, Adelle fired aimlessly again, and Noah leaped toward her. They struggled while Watts snatched the tire iron from the floor and came at Laney.

She yelped and flung the spray can at him. He

dodged, and she charged out the door, pelting toward the woods. Heavy footsteps pounded after her.

Another gunshot sounded from the cabin, echoed by a male cry of pain. *Noah! Oh, Noah!*

Laney reached the tree line and leaped over encroaching undergrowth to enter the woods. Her thrashing progress was a fatal giveaway to her location. But then, so was his. She had to find someplace to hide and plan an ambush with the knife still clutched in her fist.

A faint deer track beckoned for the quieter passage it offered, and she took it. To her left, the river gurgled, but tangled bushes hid the water from view. A dip in the earth beneath the branches caught her eye. She plopped onto her stomach and crawled under the thick foliage. Branches snagged her hair and clothes and clawed her face, but she didn't stop until she was snug and concealed, facing the path she'd just left.

"Oh, Laney, darling," a masculine voice sing-songed. "Come out, and I'll take you to your daughter." Watts's footsteps approached. "And your sister, too. You know I killed Gracie, don't you?"

A shocked cry filled her throat, but Laney held it at bay between clenched teeth. Watts killed Gracie? He was a kid at the time. Did he find out about his dad's affair and decide to punish the other woman by killing her child? That seemed more like sophisticated, though twisted, adult reasoning.

"Are you surprised?" Watts drew closer at a slug's pace. He had to know she was hiding somewhere because the sound of her movements had ceased. He'd be watching, listening for any hint of her presence.

"Would you like to know why, dear Laney?"

She swallowed and readied her knife for a strike. He was taunting her. Hoping to make her lose her head to her emotions, and he was doing a good job of it. Sweat trickled from her hairline down her nose and stung her eyes.

"I know you can hear me," he continued softly. "Grace was a pain. Always throwing fits over nothing. And stupid, too." His foot snapped a branch, and Laney flinched. He was close, but not close enough yet.

Watts chuckled. "I told her I had a whole box of her favorite candy, but she had to come with me on my bike to get it. We went out to the caves and walked up the trail. She kept whining for the candy." He snorted. "It was supposed to be a joke, but she didn't get jokes, you know. I was just going to leave her there. Serve her right. But she clawed at me, and I gave her a little smack across the cheek. Just to shut her up, you understand."

A soft pat on the trail betrayed another step closer to where she hid. Laney trembled. Every nerve-ending screamed *attack!* Not yet. Wait.

"How was I to know she'd turn and run straight over the edge of the ravine? She cracked her skull open, and it was her own stupid fault."

The brown lace-ups came into view through miniscule gaps between leaves.

"I didn't know what to do," Watts continued, "but Mom did. She said hiding the body was just the thing. She'd found out what scum you Thompsons are. In Dad's shop, she discovered the paperwork on this little love nest he bought, and a romantic note from him to your mother. Wasn't my mom clever not to let on she knew until after the FBI and your family left town?" He eased forward. "And you know what? Destiny brought you across our path so we can finish the job. Mom and I are going to cut off the generations of your family forever."

He took another step, and Laney ripped the reins off her self-control. Snarling, she pounced and plunged the knife toward his crippled foot. *Snap!* The blade met solid resistance and broke. Half in, half out of the bushes, she stared at the stub of knife in her hand.

"It's prosthetic, Sweetcakes. All the way to the knee." Watts grabbed her by the hair and dragged her to her feet, delivering a sharp slap to her cheek with his other hand.

Scalp and cheek stinging, Laney's clawed fingers sought his grinning face, but he held her at arm's length, and she came up short. She drew her foot back and rammed a kick into his right leg just below the knee. Something cracked and buckled, and Watts tumbled sideways, yelping, into the bushes.

Laney tore up the deer track the way she had come. She had to find Noah, make sure he was all right. Adelle hadn't killed him, had she? Not her Noah.

"Laney!" His hale and hearty voice answered her question.

"I'm here, Noah."

He thrashed toward her and emerged onto the path in front of her. Laney flung herself into the safety of his arms. Tears flowed onto his strong shoulder.

He petted her hair. "Hush now. It's all right."

But it wasn't. Where was Briana?

Laney lifted her head and gazed up into his loving face. "Watts killed Gracie. It was a prank gone bad. Adelle engineered the rest."

Noah nodded. "You don't have to worry about her anymore. She's tied up back at the cabin." He jerked his head in that direction.

"Watts is that way." She pointed down the deer track. "I think I broke something on his prosthetic leg."

His eyebrows climbed. "You never cease to amaze me, woman. He won't get far one-sided. I'll go truss him to a tree." He wagged a piece of rope dangling from his hand.

A patch of red on the side of his shirt caught Laney's eye. "You're hurt!"

"Just a scratch across the ribs. Burns like someone rubbed a cut with jalepeno peppers, but I'll live." He shrugged. "You've lost a lock of hair."

Laney gasped and felt the side of her head. Sure enough, a patch of her hair was missing below the ear. "Wow! That bullet came closer than I thought."

Noah chuckled. "At the moment, it's the cutest haircut I've ever seen. I sure don't want to contemplate the alternative."

"Me, either." Laney shuddered. "Say, what do you suppose happened to George?"

"His body wasn't lying in the yard, so I suspect he high-tailed it toward town and Bucky's Bar as fast as his wobbly legs could carry him." Noah sent her a muted smile. "You go call the cavalry while I round up Watts."

Laney wrinkled her nose. "As in Agent Burns?"

"I know you're desperate to find Briana. I am, too. They've got trained interrogators for our pair of slimeballs. But if they won't talk, the feds know how to throw a first rate search party. Don't worry." He touched her cheek. "We'll find her."

Laney nodded, gnawing her lower lip. But would they find her little girl alive?

NINETEEN

Why couldn't the horror end? Laney thrashed through undergrowth toward the cabin clearing. The mystery was solved, the monsters caught, and yet Briana was missing and Grace's remains were not recovered. Just wait until she got back to that cabin. She'd throttle the answer out of Adelle. She'd—

Laney burst free of the forest into the clearing. She halted and her jaw dropped. A sheriff's SUV and a pair of dark sedans filled the area. Law enforcement personnel traipsed in and out of the cabin.

"There she is," one cried and pointed in her direction.

A man in a suit broke away from the pack and strode toward her. Burns.

"Where's Ryder?" The agent glared. "He's got a lot to answer for."

"Riiight. Like finding me and saving my life. If he'd left the matter in your hands, you would have arrived in the nick of time to recover my dead body. I'm fine, by the way. You'll find the very much alive Watts Addison tied up in the woods." She jerked a thumb over her shoulder, and then planted her hands on her hips. "Now, what are you going to do to find my daughter?"

"Brianaaaaa!"

Laney's plaintive cry sliced another wound in Noah's heart. They'd searched and called, and called and searched for two hours steady. Her voice was going hoarse, and the light of hope was dying in her eyes. If only he could promise her they'd find the little princess, but he'd seen too many cases where the ending wasn't happy.

Dear Lord, please, don't let this be one of them.

The FBI did have a first class operation running, neat search grids, dogs, helicopters. But no one had found a trace of Briana, and the perps they had in custody weren't talking. Noah hadn't told Laney, but he was pretty sure the feds figured they were looking for a body, not a live child. From his own experience, he had to agree that the odds were heavily that way.

Laney plodded through the woods beside him, shoulders slumped. She called Briana's name one more time. No answer but wind in the trees and the distant *whump* of helicopter blades. They came to a fallen log, and Laney sank onto it.

She bunched her fists and pressed them to her face. "I hate her!"

Noah sat down beside her. "Adelle? Yes, she's despicable."

He wanted to add a caution against allowing bitterness and anger to warp her the same way, but Laney needed to vent honest emotions. Besides, right about now he'd pay big money for five minutes alone with the woman or her rat-faced son, and no holds barred.

Laney looked away and stared at the ground. "No, I mean my mother. None of this would have happened if she'd kept her marriage vows."

He nodded. *God, give me wisdom.* "That's true, but it's not the whole picture."

Laney issued a sour snicker. "You got that right. Then there's me leaving Grace alone to be picked on by the neighbor kid we trusted. And me again, leaving Briana behind so I could chase down leads hundreds of miles away." She sat up stiff. "If I'd been sleeping in the bed next to her, Watts couldn't have gotten to her."

Noah frowned and scuffed his toe through a mound of moldy leaves. "Are you sure about that? I tend to think you'd be dead, and Briana would still be gone. These people weren't about to let anything stop them."

Her lips spread in a grim smile. "But we did. Only it was too late." She slumped again.

He gripped her shoulders and turned her to face him. "I don't know about you, but I've sensed a divine hand guiding us through this trial." The words spilling from his lips surprised him. He'd always relied on his own wits, but he'd prayed more over this case than any other, and answers had always come—many times from unexpected quarters. "I'm not ready to give up," he told Laney. "Not by a long shot. But I'm also not prepared to watch you make the same mistake as Adelle. I couldn't bear to see your fineness turn to rot and misery."

She pulled away. "What do you mean?"

"You're a special woman, Laney. Caring, gentle, giving. You have a lot to offer the world." *And me.* "You can stay that way and go on to have a life— no matter how this search turns out—or you can go down Adelle's path, and live as pure poison to yourself and others."

Her eyes stared toward a wall of trees ahead of them. "You mean, I have to forgive my mother."

"And yourself."

She turned a desperate gaze on him. "How do I do that?"

Noah spread his hands. "Believe me, I'm no expert, but I'm guessing you choose it, in spite of your feelings, one moment at a time."

"Have you forgiven yourself for what happened to Renee?"

"I'm going to." He expelled a breath. "Right now, I choose to let it go." With the words, an airy sensation expanded his chest.

"And Burns? Have you forgiven him?"

A laugh spurted between his lips. "I suppose I need to do that, too."

"But forgiving him doesn't make him any less of a blockhead."

"You got that right." He opened his arms to her, and she melted into them. "I love you, Laney." He kissed the top of her head.

"I love you, too, Noah. I've known that for a long time, but especially when I saw your face in that cabin when I was sure I was about to die." She sat back. "Now, if we could only find Briana alive. But if not…" She gripped his hand. "Could we pray together? Right now?"

"Sure." He put his arm around her shoulder, drew her close, and they bowed their heads.

"Father God," Laney started, "I've been really angry with You for a long time. But now, I'm at the end of my ro-ope." Her voice cracked, and Noah pulled her closer. "I think I've always known that blaming You for people's evil actions was silly, so I want You to know that I choose…to forgive You. And I ask You to forgive me, too." She paused, and her shoulders heaved. "And I forgive my mom. I don't understand why Gracie's gone, or where Briana is, but You know. I'm giving them to You now." Sobs replaced words on her lips.

"God, You know I haven't been all that faithful to follow You the way my parents taught me." Noah took over praying. "I figured doing my best to be a good man was enough. I don't think that so much anymore. I think I need lots of forgiveness and mercy from You, just like everybody else. So if You'll have me, I'd like to be Your man now, not just my own." He took a deep breath. "If little Briana is in heaven with You, then she's got the best Father already, but if not, I'd consider it the highest privilege if You and Laney would let me be her earthly Daddy." Laney stirred in his arms and kissed his chin. His pulse gave a *kabump*. He'd take that as a yes from her. "In that case, we need to find her, and we need Your help. We thank You in advance for Your answer. Amen."

"Amen," Laney echoed. She rose, not releasing his hand, and tugged him after her. "Let's go find Bree."

Laney glanced at the strong profile of the man beside her on the deer track. They'd been searching and calling for another ten minutes with no results but a few more mosquito bites. Noah looked so calm, so confident, while her stomach churned.

For that brief instant of prayer, she'd felt an incredible release in choosing to forgive and to trust. But with every passing minute, worries and fears battered her emotions. Frowning, she followed Noah up the path. The battle was in her thoughts and feelings, but did that mean she had to give up on faith? No! To preserve her sanity, she had to hang on to God and the man He'd sent her way for a time like this.

Ahead, the river gurgled, and they emerged on the bank. A figure sat slumped on a rock at water's edge.

"George Addison," Laney murmured.

Noah led the way over to him. "Happy to see you're all right."

The man stood and faced them. "Likewise. No thanks to me." His complexion was pasty pale, and his eyes bloodshot, but the strong gaze and firm set of his jaw spoke a sobriety Laney hadn't seen in him since her childhood.

"I'm a mess," he pronounced. "I don't know how I let myself get this bad." He lowered his gaze. "Sorry for running off like that, but I wasn't thinking too clear."

"You were also being shot at." Laney stepped toward him. This man was much more like the neighbor she'd liked.

George examined his fingers. "Did they get away?"

"No, they're in custody," Noah said.

George nodded and sighed. "It's for the best. They had to be stopped. I'm going to visit him, you know." He looked up at them.

"Visit?" Laney blinked.

"In prison. I'm going to see Watts as often as I can. So he turned out to be a rotten human being. Like I should judge." He snorted. "He's still my son. And as long as there's life, there's hope. Isn't that the saying?"

Laney's chest tightened. As long as there's life…
Was there really any hope of finding Briana still
breathing? Noah squeezed Laney's arm as if he
knew what she was thinking. She shot him a
grateful look.

"Maybe you can help us out, George," he said.
"Would you know of any hiding places around
here? Somewhere they could stash a little girl?"

George responded with a blank stare. "The kid's
still missing?"

Laney's heart sank to her toes. They'd never find
her daughter. Briana would remain close to them
only in their memories…like Gracie.

Then George's face brightened. "Say, come to
think of it, when I bought the property, I noticed
an old root cellar marked on the plat map."

Laney rushed forward and grabbed the man's
arm. "Where, George, where?"

He scratched the back of his head. "I'm not too
clear on the exact spot, but it was somewhere
behind the cabin near the river. I never went
looking for it myself."

Noah whipped out his cell phone. "I'll notify the
searchers to converge in that area. Laney, we're
going to find that cellar. I promise you."

Laney's breath snagged. Yes, they had to locate
the cellar, but what would they find in it?

Eternal minutes turned into an awful hour, as
searchers crawled like ants over every square inch

of the forestation behind the cabin. Noah stamped his foot on the earth beneath his feet, listening for the hollow sound that would betray a cavity below. Nearby, but unseen in the trees, men's voices called as they cleared brush and checked grid areas. If Adelle and Watts had used the cellar as a hiding place, they had hidden the entrance well.

A few feet from Noah, Laney made the same stamping motions he did. Her face was drawn, gaze fevered, hope stretched to the limit. They neared the edge of the tree line. Not far away a steep slope led down to the river. Noah approached the lip of the slope, and a sizeable patch of moldering leaves caught his eye. The area was roughly square and shadowed beneath the massive branches of an oak tree. Had someone spread the leaves to mask a spot of earth they didn't want discovered?

Noah eased over in that direction, watching Laney from the corner of his eye. She was absorbed in checking an area farther upriver. He didn't want to get her hopes up until he could confirm that he'd found something. As he neared the suspicious spot, he noted that the leaves seemed raised an inch or so above the other forest floor mulch. His heart rate went into overdrive. He lifted his foot and brought it down on the edge of the leaf mound. A woody *thunk* answered him.

Noah closed his eyes, and a hot tear traced a path down one cheek. *Thank You, God. Now make us strong to bear whatever we find.*

"Here!" he cried. "It's here!"

A feminine shriek announced that Laney had heard. Noah got on the phone and notified the search coordinator as Laney rushed up beside him. She fell to her knees and began sweeping leaves away, saying, "Oh, God, please," over and over again. Noah closed his phone and helped her remove the debris. Soon, a set of paintless and rotting cellar doors was revealed. The sound of voices said the other searchers were drawing near.

Laney lunged for the rusty handles, but Noah pulled her back.

"Let me go!" She wriggled against him.

"We'll go together, but we'll go with caution. The wood is rotten, and we have no idea if there are critters down there that won't take kindly to intrusion." Noah beat back a mental picture of a dead or drugged Briana at the mercy of a carnivorous animal.

Laney's face went pasty-pale. She was a bright girl. She'd glimpsed the same vision he had.

"Stand aside!" Burns's strident tone broke them apart. "This is a potential crime scene. We'll take it from here."

The lead agent reached them, along with a couple of other agents and sheriff's department searchers.

Laney marched up to Burns and stuck her face in his. "You'll have to arrest me to keep me from going down to look for my daughter. And if you do,

I wonder how that will look in the newspapers—FBI Jails Distraught Mother of Abducted Child."

Burns's mouth came open but no sound came out. She'd pushed a major hot button, and she knew it. Noah suppressed a snicker.

"Noah and I are going to see if my daughter is down there." She poked him in the chest. "If she's awake and scared all alone in the dark, we're going to be the first people she sees. After that, you can set up housekeeping in the cellar for all I care."

"Miss Thompson," Burns said with exaggerated patience, "an agent *is* going down with you. Evidence must be protected."

"Send as many as you like, but Briana is not evidence. We're going down now." She turned away and marched toward Noah.

He nodded to her and pulled the handle on one of the doors. It was more solid and heavy than it looked, and the hinges creaked a loud protest. The darkness below exhaled a musty odor, but not the smell of a decomposing carcass. Of course, if Adelle and Watts had killed Briana, she wouldn't have been dead long enough to stink. A steep and narrow set of wooden stairs led downward, another hazard if any of them were rotten.

Noah grabbed Laney's hand. The little member was clammy and trembled. Bold as a lion to the pretentious agent, but petrified of what the next few minutes might hold. He didn't blame her.

He brought her fingers to his lips. "Me first."

She nodded without a word.

Noah held out a hand toward one of the searchers who had a flashlight on his belt. "Mind if I use that?"

The man gave it to him. "Good luck."

Pointing the beam down onto the steps, Noah tried the first one. It groaned but held, and he descended another and another. Laney followed so close behind him her warm breath feathered against his neck. He glanced over his shoulder at a third set of footfalls on the stairs. Burns himself, scowling as dark as the pit below them.

Noah proceeded and, a few steps later, reached a packed earth floor. He panned the flashlight around the area. Empty shelves lined the walls, some of them broken and tumbled into splintered junk, but others intact. Laney gasped and clutched his arm as he halted the light on an odd-shaped mound on the floor in the corner. Burns darted ahead of them, holding a forestalling palm in their direction. They crept forward anyway.

Noah stared down at the forlorn heap of bones and hair clothed in moldering jeans and what might once have been a red shirt.

"Gracie!"

Laney's soft wail melted his heart.

"We found you. Oh, we found you at last." The words tumbled from Laney's lips. She should be sad, but a fierce joy blazed through her blood. Then ice chilled her veins. "Briana!" She whirled, staring wildly around the room.

Noah's arm came around her, clasping her tight, steadying her. The light streaming from his hand darted here, then there, then the far corner beyond the steps. There lay another mound, small and oddly shaped, like the one they'd just found. As one, they rushed forward. At the last second, Noah inserted himself in front of her and held her back.

"It's Bree!" She swatted at him, but he caught her hand.

"Let me check her first."

Chest heaving, throat nearly closed, she managed a nod. He turned and knelt beside the little girl in pink princess pajamas who lay motionless in a fetal position in the dirt. Briana's thick brown hair spread in a cloud around her head. Her sweet profile, pale as glass, was angelically peaceful. In death or sleep? Laney held her breath as Noah leaned over her daughter and touched her throat under the jawbone where a pulse should be.

Had to be!

Then Noah looked at her, and his face burst into a brilliant grin. He scooped Briana up and thrust her into Laney's reaching arms. "She's okay!" His triumphant laugh filled the dark pit.

Laney cuddled the warm body of her slumbering daughter and laughed and cried as Noah's arms came around them both, cradling Briana between them. Her daughter stirred, and Laney looked down to find the little eyelids fluttering.

"She's waking up. Oh, thank You, Jesus!"

"Amen!" Noah bent and placed a kiss on Briana's forehead.

The child's eyes flipped open wide, but she didn't focus on her mother. Instead, Briana's groggy smile was aimed at Noah.

"I knew my daddy would find me."

TWENTY

"Stop that fighting, boys!" Laney stepped between two fourth grade hooligans who had taken swings at each other on the playground. "It's barely a week into the school year, and you're not getting off to a wise start."

They glared at each other, then scowled up at her.

"We're headed straight for the principal's office." She wagged a finger at them, and their gazes dropped. "March!"

"Aw!" One of them protested, as she herded them toward the door.

Laney ushered them inside, up the hallway, and into the outer administration office.

Miss Aggie looked up from her work and sent the youngsters a strong stare. "You two again?" She looked at Laney. "I'll get Mr. Ryder."

The boys studied the toes of their sneakers.

A moment later, Noah strode out of his inner sanctum, stern gaze fixed on the pair of would-be

Rocky Balboas. He crooked a finger in their direction, and they dragged their feet toward his office. The principal ushered them inside, then, hand on his doorknob, turned and winked at Laney.

She blew him a kiss, and a beam of sunlight from the window behind Miss Aggie's desk sent sparks dancing from the rock on her left ring finger—right next to the wedding band that had been a fixture for the past five weeks.

"I saw that." Ellen Kline's voice came from over by the teacher mailboxes.

Laney laughed and hooked arms with her friend. As they headed out the door, she waved at Miss Aggie. The woman's understated smile radiated a blessing.

"You know what I think," Ellen said as they proceeded up the hall. "Noah puts kids up to those antics so he can catch a glimpse of his new bride."

"Oh, you!" Laney giggled, cheeks warming.

The school board had been relieved that their star principal decided to continue serving the district, rather than returning to his former career. But like Noah said, private investigator was no occupation for a family man. Approval of their marriage had been universal on their return to Cottonwood Grove in safety and triumph—except for a few jealous looks from several single women in the area. She sympathized with them. Noah was quite a catch, but he was all hers. Well, not quite.

She smiled as she returned to playground duty. She knew a little girl who couldn't get enough of her new daddy. Laney could almost be jealous if she weren't so deliriously happy.

* * * * *

Dear Reader,

I hope you had to hang on to your seat throughout the thrills and chills of mortal danger with Noah Ryder, Laney Thompson and little Briana.

I enjoyed setting the tale in localities of rural Minnesota. As a resident of such a rural area, I'm familiar with the idiosyncrasies of our unique subculture. The Pantry Café is a real institution in my hometown (yes, the pancakes are bigger than the plate), as are people like Mr. Bingham. And it is not uncommon to see empty vehicles left running in the grocery store parking lot in the dead of winter.

The subject of child abduction, or child abuse of any kind, is dear to my heart. I have a passion for teaching, training and protecting children, much like the main characters in the story. If you have an opportunity to support programs that protect children, as well as those that seek the lost, I urge you to do so. You can find more information at the National Center for Missing and Exploited Children (www.missingkids.com) or the National Child Safety Council (www.national-childsafetycouncil.org) and other fine child protection groups.

As always, Dear Reader, you are invited to visit

me at www.jillelizabethnelson.com for ongoing book giveaways, updates, and excerpts of current and coming releases.

Abundant Blessings to you and yours,

Jill Elizabeth Nelson

QUESTIONS FOR DISCUSSION

1. Laney's past comes back to haunt her in the form of her sister's backpack. Have you ever had the unexpected appearance of a physical object or person carry you back to a significant moment in your past?

2. A past trauma spurred Noah to make a drastic career change. Name a pivotal moment in your own life and what changed.

3. Guilt haunts Laney and Noah. How are their reasons for feeling guilty similar? How are they different? Are their reasons valid?

4. What methods are Laney and Noah using to deal with their guilt? When you experience guilty feelings, how do you deal with them? Name healthy ways to deal with guilt—real or perceived.

5. Sometimes we encounter difficult people. At times, these are the very people we would expect to provide solutions rather than obstacles. Who is this person in Laney and Noah's lives? If this has ever happened to you, how did you deal with the issue?

6. Briana's innocent faith provides encouragement to the adults in her life. Can you name a time when a child provided the inspiration you needed to get through a problem?

7. Laney instinctively trusts Noah and is drawn to him romantically, even though Pierce seems a more sensible choice. Has your instinct ever argued with your intellect? Which voice did you listen to, and how did the situation turn out?

8. Noah is a strong, decisive man, but the death of his fiancée devastated him. When Laney's situation arises, does he revert to self-sufficiency or acknowledge his insufficiency and call upon God? Are you a more self-reliant or God-reliant person?

9. The Thompson family had decided not to tell Briana about her murdered Aunt Grace until she was older. Have you ever faced a situation when you had to decide how much or what to tell a child about a difficult issue?

10. Laney's parents keep a major secret from their daughter. If the secret had not connected to the threats on Laney and Briana, do you think such knowledge about a parent should be shared with the offspring? Why or why not?

11. Our sin can have far-reaching affects on others. Can you name a time when a wrong thing you did impacted someone innocent? Or a time when something someone else did negatively impacted your life? How can these issues be addressed?

12. Why did George and Adelle's marriage fall apart and Roland and Loretta's heal and grow stronger?

13. Bitterness twisted Adelle into a woman capable of doing anything to get revenge. Does retribution bring permanent satisfaction? When have you been tempted to "get back" at someone? Did you follow through? Why or why not, and what was the result of your choice?

14. In her anger, Laney could become another Adelle. What particular act saves her from going down that road?

15. Noah takes baby steps of faith throughout the story. What conscious decision about God does he make at the end? Does that decision make him better daddy and husband material?

Here's a sneak peek at
THE WEDDING GARDEN
by Linda Goodnight,
the second book in her new miniseries
REDEMPTION RIVER,
available in May 2010 from Love Inspired.

One step into the living room and she froze again, pan aloft.

A hulking shape stood in shadow just inside the French doors leading out to the garden veranda. This was not Popbottle Jones. This was a big, bulky, dangerous-looking man. She raised the pan higher.

"What do you want?"

"Annie?" He stepped into the light.

All the blood drained from Annie's face. Her mouth went dry as saltines. "Sloan Hawkins?"

The man removed a pair of silver aviator sunglasses and hung them on the neck of his black rock-and-roll T-shirt. He'd rolled the sleeves up, baring muscular biceps. A pair of eyes too blue to define narrowed, looking her over as though he were a wolf and she a bunny rabbit.

Annie suppressed an annoying shiver.

It was Sloan, all right, though older and with more muscle. His nearly black hair was shorter now—no more bad-boy curl over the forehead—but bad boy screamed off him in waves just the same. He was devastatingly handsome, in a tough, rugged, manly kind of way. The years had been kind to Sloan Hawkins.

She really wanted to hate him, but she'd already wasted too much emotion on this outlaw. With God's help she'd learned to forgive. But she wasn't about to forget.

Will Sloan and Annie's faith be
strong enough to see them through
the pain of the past and allow them
to open their hearts to a possible future?
Find out in THE WEDDING GARDEN
by Linda Goodnight,
available May 2010 from Love Inspired.